A Book of Spooks and Spectres

A BOOK OF

SPOOKS AND SPECTRES

Ruth Manning-Sanders

ILLUSTRATED BY

ROBIN JACQUES

E. P. DUTTON NEW YORK

First published in the U.S.A. 1980 by E. P. Dutton,
a Division of Elsevier-Dutton Publishing Company,
Inc., New York.

Library of Congress Cataloging in Publication Data

Manning-Sanders, Ruth, date. A book of spooks and spectres.
SUMMARY: Twenty-three ghostly tales from around the world.
1. Tales. 2. Ghost stories. [1. Folklore. 2. Ghost stories] I. Jacques, Robin. II. Title.
PZ8.1.M298Bnh 398.2'5 79-17673 ISBN: 0-525-27045-0

Printed in the U.S.A. First Edition
10 9 8 7 6 5 4 3 2 1

Contents

For permission to retell Goralasi and the Spectres *the author wishes to thank Messrs Erich Röth – Verlag, Kassel.*

Introduction to Spooks and Spectres

If you were to meet a Spook and a Spectre walking together, would you know which was which? Not necessarily. Both are ghostly beings, and you might possibly mistake one for the other. Yet there is a great difference. Spooks have always been Spooks; they have a king to rule over them, and a country of their own.

Spectres, on the other hand, have not always been Spectres. They were once creatures of flesh and blood, generally human beings, who after death, find the gates of heaven and hell shut against them, and so must return to earth. Sometimes these Spectres settle down together and enjoy themselves – you will read about a merry company of them in the Korean story, *Yi Chang and the Spectres.* But more often they are unhappy solitaries, like *Tummeldink*, the proud rich man, who, thinking he has enough of everything, scorns God's reward, and so when he dies cannot enter heaven: or like the wretched Spectre in the German story, *The Inn of the Stone and Spectre*, who is forever trying to put back the boundary stone which, when he was a man of flesh and blood, he had dishonestly moved to his own advantage.

On the whole, I should say that Spooks are happy beings, and Spectres unhappy ones. What more doleful than the spectral youths and maidens in the *Dance of the Spectres* – a story from Savoy? What more merry and mischievous than the Spooks in the Danish story *The Spook and the Beer Barrel*, or those in the American story *La-lee-lu*, or the rascally little bird Spook in the German story *Ha! ha! ha!* But of course there are exceptions: for instance the Spook in the charming Icelandic story *Dilly-dilly-doh* is anything but a happy being, whereas the Spectres in the Australian story, *Goralasi and the Spectres*, seem happy enough.

Well, here, to wind up, are two little anecdotes, one in verse, the other in prose:

Anecdote One:

The other day upon the stair
I met a man who wasn't there
I met the man again today –
And oh I wish *he'd go away!*

Anecdote Two:

Two men are sitting opposite each other in a railway carriage. Mr A, facing the engine, is reading a book. Mr B, with his back to the engine, is looking dreamily out of the window. Suddenly Mr A claps his book shut and exclaims 'Pah! I don't believe in Spectres!'

'Oh don't you?' says Mr B . . . And vanishes.

Well, the man in the railway carriage who vanishes is undoubtedly a Spectre. But that tiresome fellow on the stairs – is he a Spectre or is he a Spook? I don't know. Can any of you tell me?

1 · *Old Tommy and the Spectre*

Once upon a time, and a long time ago, a Spectre went wandering through the country looking for a place to live. And on the border, just where England ends and Wales begins, he found the very house he was looking for. It was a pretty house, not too big and not too small; it had a garden with rose bushes and apple trees, and it was handsomely furnished.

The owner of the house, Mr Jones, didn't live in it (he was a merchant and lived in town) but of course he didn't want to keep the house empty. So he decided to let it.

And he did let it; he let it over and over again; but no one would stay in it. Well, how could you expect people to stay, when they couldn't so much as go upstairs without meeting the Spectre coming down? And if they went into the library in the evening, like as not they would see the Spectre seated at the table, turning over the leaves of some big book or other, and muttering to himself. He was enough to scare anyone out of his wits, was that Spectre, with his bluish-whitish body that you could see through, his nodding head, his long green hair, his pale staring eyes, his beak of a nose, and his great mouth with no lips to it. Add to all this that though he had legs and feet, he didn't walk – he *floated*.

Mr Jones got so annoyed about the Spectre that he felt like burning the house down. But his wife said, 'Why don't you send for old Tommy?'

'Old Tommy,' says Mr Jones, 'who's he?'

'He's an old fellow who lives in the village,' says Mrs Jones. 'People say he has a way with Spectres. He sent one packing out of Robinson's farm, so I'm told.'

So Mr Jones went to call on old Tommy, whom he found in his garden, digging up potatoes.

'Tommy,' says Mr Jones, 'I've a job for you. And if you can make a success of it, I'll pay you handsomely.'

'What's the job then?' says old Tommy.

'To get rid of an unwelcome guest,' says Mr Jones.

And he tells Tommy about the Spectre.

Old Tommy leans on his spade and looks at Mr Jones. There's a twinkle in his bright blue eyes. 'I'll have a try at him, sir,' says he. 'I'll go up to the house tonight. Let me have a good blazing fire in that there liber-rary of yours, and a bottle full of brandy and a glass, and maybe a sandwich or two; and also an empty bottle with a good cork to it, and a stick of sealing wax. Don't forget about the empty bottle and the cork and the sealing wax, for they be the most important of all.'

'And you think you can get rid of the thing?' says Mr Jones, greatly relieved.

'Sir,' says Tommy. 'I don't say as I *can*. All I say is I'll *try*.'

So that evening, there was old Tommy seated in an armchair before a bright fire in the library. On a table at his side were the two bottles, one filled with brandy, the other empty, and also a plate holding a plentiful supply of ham sandwiches. For some reason best known to himself Tommy had locked the library door and put the key in his pocket. He had also taken the cork out of the empty bottle and laid it on the table.

'Now,' says he with a chuckle, 'you can come just as soon as you've a mind to, my friend!'

For a long time nobody did come. It was all very quiet-seeming: just the little tick-tock of the clock on the mantelpiece (which Tommy had wound up) and the soft-sounding flare of the small flames in the fire. Tommy had eaten a sandwich or two, and had taken more than a few sips out of the brandy bottle. Now his head kept nodding and his eyes kept shutting; he was in danger of falling asleep, which of course would never do. He was giving himself a good pinch, when he felt a kind of breezy stir in the air behind him, and glancing over his shoulder he saw the Spectre moving without a sound across the floor.

The Spectre was taller than the tallest man Tommy had ever

seen. He had long locks of green hair, and he had nothing on him that you could call anything: only some wisps of bluish-whitish floating clouds. But he had a voice that seemed to fill the whole room, for it was as loud as a storm of wind.

'Well, old Tommy,' says the Spectre in that roaring voice of his. 'And how do you find yourself this evening?'

'In the pink,' says Tommy. 'But how do you come to know my name?'

'Oh, easy enough,' says the Spectre.

'But I haven't the pleasure of knowing yours,' says old Tommy.

'I don't own to one,' says the Spectre. 'Call me what you please.'

'Well then, Mr What-You-Please,' says Tommy, 'how did you get in here? Not by the door, I do know, because I locked it.'

'I got in through the keyhole,' says the Spectre.

'Oh no, Mr What-You-Please,' says Tommy. 'I'm not believing that! A great fellow like you couldn't get through a keyhole!'

'I tell you I *did* get through the keyhole!' says the Spectre, in that loud roaring stormy-windy voice of his.

Tommy shakes his head. He puts on a very serious unbelieving look. 'It's no laughing matter when a fellow tells lies,' says he.

'*Lies*, *LIES!*' roars the Spectre, and now his voice was louder than a thunder clap. 'WHO'S TELLING LIES?'

'You needn't deafen me,' says Tommy. 'But you know, a size of a fellow such as you be, to get through a keyhole, just as if you were an ant or a fly – why, it don't make sense! I'd as soon believe you could get into this empty bottle here on the table.'

'So I can get into it,' roars the Spectre.

'Don't believe it,' says Tommy.

'I *can*, I *CAN*,' roars the Spectre.

'Don't believe it,' says Tommy again.

'IS SEEING BELIEVING THEN OR IS IT NOT?' roars the Spectre.

And next moment he shrank to the size of a match stick and gave a skip into the bottle.

In a flash Tommy snatched up the cork and rammed it down into

BRAND

the neck of the bottle. Then he took the stick of sealing wax from the table. He heated the wax at a candle flame till it was dripping all over the place; and then he covered the cork with the melted wax. He made the sign of the cross on the hot wax – and burned his fingers in the doing of it – but what of that? Now, with the bottle tucked under his arm, he was scurrying off out of the house, and down to the bank of a near by river.

The river was swift-flowing and deep. 'Catch as catch can!' shouted Tommy. And he flung the bottle out into the water. For a moment he watched it, bobbing away on the surface of the water. Then it sank. 'Just as if someone had pulled it down,' said Tommy to himself.

'A pleasant journey to you, Mr Spectre!' says he, laughing. 'I'm not particular where the bottle carries you, so long as it don't bring you here no more!'

And he waved his hand to the river, and turned and went back into the house.

And where did that bottle go? Some people say that it is still lying at the bottom of the river. Others say that the river carried it down to the sea, and that the sea washed it up on to the shore, and that a girl picked it up and opened it, and wished she hadn't. Others, again, say that the bottle, with the Spectre inside it, is to this day washing about in the sea, somewhere between Wales and Ireland.

Anyway, one thing is certain. The Spectre never came back to Mr Jones's house.

In his gratitude, Mr Jones offered to let old Tommy live in the house rent free. But Tommy said, 'Me? What should I do with that great building round my neck? I'd rather you put me to work in the garden.'

So then Mr Jones made Tommy head gardener: which meant that he had a good wage, and a cottage to live in, rent free. And no hard work to do, either, only to boss it over two brisk lads whom Mr Jones put to work under him.

Old Tommy told the two lads all about his adventure with the Spectre. And the two lads told it to their sweethearts. And when they married, the wives told it to their children. And when the children grew up and married they told it to *their* children. So the story was never forgotten. And that is how I am now able to tell it to you.

2 · *La-lee-lu*

Well now, there were twelve little Spooks who got tired of living in Spook Land. So they changed themselves into a flock of geese, and went flying about to see the world.

And as they were flying they were singing a merry nonsense song: '*La-lee-lu, come quilla, come quilla, bung, bung, bung, quilla bung.*'

Flap, flap, flap: now they were flying over a cottage where a man lived with his wife. And when the man heard that, *La-lee-lu*, he looked out of the door, and saw the geese flying *flip-flap, flip-flap*. So he said to his wife, 'Ho, ho, now we can have roast goose for dinner.'

Then he took his gun, went out, shot one of the geese, and carried it in to his wife.

The wife began to pluck the goose; and each feather, as she plucked it off, flew out of the window.

That startled her, but never mind. When she had finished plucking the goose she laid it all tidy on a baking dish and put the dish in the oven.

And all the time that the goose was cooking, a muffled voice was coming out of the oven, singing, '*La-lee-lu, come quilla, come quilla, bung, bung, bung, quilla bung.*'

Well, when the goose was cooked, the wife dished it up, and put it on the table. But when the man took up a knife and fork to carve it, I'm blessed if it didn't begin to sing again, '*La-lee-lu, come quilla, come quilla, bung, bung, bung, quilla bung.*'

'Be quiet, can't you?' said the man. And he was just about to stick his fork into the goose, when there came a tremendous noise, and the whole flock of geese flew in through the window singing, '*La-lee-lu, come quilla, come quilla, bung, bung, bung, quilla bung!*'

The song was a bit muffled, because each of the geese was carrying a lot of feathers in its beak. And now they were all sticking those feathers into the goose on the dish. Then the goose stood up in the dish, flapping its wings, and the whole flock of them flew out of the window and went back to Spook Land, singing, '*La-lee-lu, come quilla, come quilla, bung, bung, bung, quilla bung.*'

3 · *Football on a Lake*

The two Chans, father and son, were wealthy landowners who lived near a great lake. More than anything, they enjoyed boating; but they were also known throughout the country as famous footballers. Even up to the time that he was forty, father Chan went on with the game; and he might have been playing until he was sixty, if he hadn't come to a sad end, being lost in a boating accident on the lake. Nobody knew just what happened on that evening; but next day the boat was found drifting bottom upward, and of old Chan there was no trace.

For a long time after that had happened, young Chan wouldn't go near the lake; he left it to his serving boys to keep the boat in repair, and do his fishing for him. And then one moonlit evening, as he was taking a solitary walk, thinking melancholy thoughts and not heeding where he was going, he absent-mindedly wandered down to the lake close to the place where the boat was moored.

The moonlight lay along the water in a broad glittering path. Young Chan, still almost absent-mindedly, unmoored the boat, edged it into the water, jumped in, took up the oars, and rowed out along the glittering trackway of the moon.

Now all around him was silence, except for the swish, swish of the oars as they dipped and rose. And then suddenly young Chan heard a very strange flurry of noise and saw a very strange sight. Up out of the lake rose five men carrying a huge mat. They spread the mat upon the surface of the water, and then they dived down again, and came up again bringing food in silver dishes, and wine in wonderful glass goblets that shone and twinkled in the moon's rays. And when all was ready, three of the men sat down to dine, whilst the other two, an active man and a lad, waited on them.

Not one of those people took any notice of Chan, or of his boat. But Chan took notice of them; in fact he couldn't take his eyes off those three who were dining. Strangely enough, he couldn't see their faces, though of course they must have had faces! What he did see, and wonder at, was the magnificence of their clothes. One was dressed in a blue robe, two were dressed in white robes. The blue robe was sparkling with sapphires, the white robes sparkled with diamonds. All three wore big turbans on their heads, and the turbans also sparkled with jewels. And if the rainbow has seven colours, those turbans had more, and the colours kept shifting and changing so that it made young Chan feel giddy to look at them. So he turned his attention to the two servants: the active man and the lad. The lad had goggle eyes and a pouting mouth; he reminded young Chan of a carp. But when young Chan looked at the man, his heart seemed like to jump clean out of his body, for surely, surely that serving man was his father! But no, no, it couldn't be; for when the serving man spoke to the boy, giving him some sharp directions, that serving man's voice was shrill as the wind whistling through rushes, and never in his life had young Chan heard his father speak like that!

Well, by and by, when the three who were feasting had eaten and drunk their fill, one of them said, 'Now we will have a game of football! You, boy, bring up the ball.'

The boy dived down under the water, and the next moment came up again carrying a monstrous ball. It was so large that he could scarcely get his arms round it to carry it; it was transparent, but it seemed to be made of silver, glittering both inside and out. Young Chan's eyes were so dazzled that it was all he could do to look at it.

The three men got up from the table. The table, with its silver dishes, glass goblets and all, together with the mat, sank gently down under the water, and was lost to sight. The man in the blue robe turned to the serving man and said, 'Now, famous footballer, show us one of your kicks!'

The serving man took a run at the ball and gave a kick. Up went the ball twenty feet into the air, sparkling and shining. Down it came again, up it went again, the three lake men taking sides, one with the serving man, two against. Chan couldn't see any goals, and the game seemed to have no rules. It was just a scuffle, two against two, the glittering ball whirling up, bouncing down, faster, and faster, and *faster*.

Now young Chan was standing up in the boat. He was so excited that he began to shout. But nobody took any notice of him, until – well, what do you think? The ball, after an extra vigorous kick from the serving man, which seemed to send it flying up almost as high as heaven, came flying down again, and landed in the boat right at young Chan's feet. That was more than young Chan could bear: join in the game he must and would! And with a loud shout he kicked the ball as hard as he could.

But the ball was as light as a feather, and as soft as rice paper. Young Chan's foot went right through it. Still, up it went: up and up and up, with its many coloured lights streaming from the hole that Chan had made in it. And then, as swiftly as it had flown up, down it came again, until it touched the water, when it fizzed and went out.

'Well kicked, well kicked indeed!' shrilled the serving man who was so like Chan's father, yet whose voice was so different. 'Why, I remember in the old days when I was at home, and my son, young Chan, and I were famed throughout the country for – well, there, I gave such kicks as that . . . But – '

'Father, Father,' cried young Chan, 'don't you know me? Look at me, I *am* young Chan – I *am* your son.'

The serving man gave a shout of joy. He came rushing over the surface of the water towards the boat. But the three men of the lake, the men with the big turbans and the sparkling robes, were screaming with rage. Now from under those sparkling robes they drew sharp swords. They rushed across the water, waving those swords, and shrieking, 'Kill the scoundrel! Kill the scoundrel who has spoiled our game!'

Young Chan could never clearly remember what happened after that. He had drawn his own sword, he was fighting for his life, hacking away at the turbaned heads and the long white arms of the lake

men. And Chan's father was catching hold of the lake men's legs, and was dragging them away from the boat, until first one, and then another, and then the third of the lake men fell back under the water. Old Chan scrambled into the boat, plumped down in the stern and took the tiller, young Chan took the oars . . . And the next moment there they were, old Chan and young Chan, making for land.

But they were not safe yet. Suddenly a huge mouth yawned open in the lake. And out of that huge mouth came a roaring wind which lashed the water into monstrous waves. On came the huge mouth, nearer and nearer: in another moment the Chans' boat would have been swallowed, had not father Chan seized one of two great flat stones, which were kept in the boat to use as anchors, and thrown it bang into the gaping mouth. The gaping mouth, sucking on the stone as if it had been a lollipop, disappeared under the water. Then the lake became calm again, and the two Chans got safe to shore.

And if, that evening, there were any two men in this world happier than old Chan and young Chan, all I can say is that you would have to go a very long way to find them. But I doubt if they ever went boating on that lake again.

4 · *The Spooks' Party*

Once upon a time an old woman went to market and left her house empty.

By and by along comes a company of Spooks.

'Hurrah!' say they. 'Here's an empty house. Now we'll have a party!'

So they all go in, turn themselves into different kinds of creatures, and begin to dance and sing.

The Magpie sings:

'I, the Magpie, lead off the dance!'

The little Hen in high boots dances the polka. The little Duck plays the flute, the Crane begins to dance, to fling out his long legs, to stretch out his long neck.

The Goat sings:

'I, the Goat, dance in and out, my little hoofs go *trop*, *trop*, *trop*!'

The Ram sings:

'I, the Ram, beat the drum, *bop*, *bop*, *bop*!'

The Owl sings:

'I, the Owl, stamp with my feet, click with my beak, with my eyes go *pop*, *pop*, *pop!*'

But just then the old woman came back from market.

She seized a broom, and *Hoosh*! she swept them all out through the open door.

And that was the end of the Spooks' party.

5 · *Spooks a-hunting*

Every year, on Saint Martin's night, the Spooks set out to hunt in the forest. They come riding along the high road, a great company of them, with their three-footed dogs barking and yapping at the horses' heels. If you happen to be out on the road and hear them coming, you must fling yourself flat and shut your eyes. Then they will ride over you without hurting you. But woe betide you if you dare to look at them!

And when the hunt, on its way to the forest, passes through a village, the people must go into their houses, shut the doors, pull down the blinds, draw the curtains, and not venture to stir out again, or take a peep through a window, until the grand procession has gone by. For the Spooks have a great objection to prying eyes; and should you venture to look upon them, you will very likely be snatched away and never be seen again. Or so the villagers say.

Well now, the story goes that in a certain village there was a woman who had more curiosity than sense. She said that all this tale about the Spooks not wishing to be looked at was rubbish; and anyhow how were *they* to know whether they were being watched or not? She said, moreover, that she had never seen the Spooks, and she wanted to see the Spooks, and here was her chance, and she was going to take it.

So, on Saint Martin's night, though she shut her house door and drew the curtains across most of her windows, she left the window curtains in her bedroom just a little apart. Then she opened the window, blew out her candle, sat herself down behind those bedroom curtains, and, through the little gap she had left in them, peered out into the night.

What did she hear, what did she see? First of all she heard a *swish*

swish, swish, and saw a big birch broom coming along the road all by itself, and sweeping the road clean. Then she heard *clump, clump, clump*, and saw twelve big shoes stamping along without any feet in them. And after the twelve big shoes came the Wild Hunt itself: a company of great shadowy riders on great shadowy horses. The horses' feet made no sound at all as they went by at a gallop, followed by a pack of three-legged dogs with fiery eyes that lit up every bump on the road as they rushed past.

Next came a troop of tiny green mannikins, running like the wind, and screaming, 'Hopp! Hopp! Hopp!'

And lastly behind the riders and the horses and the fiery-eyed dogs and the mannikins, came, waddling all by itself, a bandy-legged goose. And when the woman saw that goose, stretching out its neck, flapping its wings and twiddling its yellow feet, hurrying in an attempt to keep up with the rest of the procession – well there, she burst out laughing.

And what did the goose do then? It stepped aside and gave a peck at the woman's garden fence. Then *flap-flap* and *twiddle-twiddle* – off with it in a hurry along the road after the riders.

'*Oh, oh, oh!*' the woman gave a shriek. For, believe it or not, though the goose had only pecked at the garden fence, the woman felt the goose's beak pecking at her left leg. If a sharp pair of scissors had been driven into her leg it couldn't have been more painful. And as the days went by, the pain didn't get any better, it got worse. She went to the doctor, and he gave her lotions and ointments to rub on her leg; she went to the priest, and he prayed over the leg – it was all no good. Lame she was, and lame she remained, for a whole year.

Then came Saint Martin's night again. The woman wasn't peeping out from between her bedroom curtains this year. Her house was in darkness; she was sitting before her kitchen fire with her sore leg up on a stool, for the pain in her leg had never been worse. So she didn't see the birch broom sweeping the road, nor the twelve big shoes stumping along, nor the shadowy riders on their shadowy horses, nor the fiery-eyed dogs, nor the green mannikins, nor the bandy-legged goose that hurried flapping its wings at the tail of the procession.

But now the goose was speaking in such a loud clear voice that even though the kitchen window was shut, and the blind down, and the curtains drawn across the blind, the woman could hear every word that the goose was saying.

And this is what it was saying, 'Last year I stuck a hook in this fence. Now I'll take it out again.'

Then the goose stepped over to the woman's garden fence, gave a peck, and pulled out something that looked like a little silver fish hook, sharp and glittering.

The goose dropped the little glittering bit of a hook on to the road. Hey presto! The hook vanished. And as it vanished the pain went from the woman's leg, and she jumped up, opened the window, and leaned out.

'Oh thank you, thank you, dear goose!' she cried.

And the goose answered:

'Eyes that see more than they should
Will never bring their owner good.
But she who's learned this lesson right
Need not fear Saint Martin's night.'

And then it waddled away along the road, with its neck stretched out and its wings flapping, in a hurry to catch up with the grand procession.

6 • *Yi Chang and the Spectres*

When Yi Chang's uncle died, he left Yi Chang a big sum of money. 'Now what shall I do with all this money?' thought Yi Chang. 'Ah, I know! I'll buy a fine house and ask my brothers Hu and Ho to live with me. That will be pleasant for me, and that will be pleasant for them. And we shall all be happy.'

So Yi Chang went into the suburbs of the town, and walked up one road and down another road, looking at the houses. Well, of course they were most of them lived in; but by and by, just where the town ended and the country began, he saw a house that had a notice FOR SALE written on a board beside the entrance gate. It was a fine big house with a great many windows, and a verandah outside the first floor windows, and a garden in the front of it, and a garden at the back of it.

'The very place, couldn't be better!' thought Yi Chang. And he went to the official entrusted with the sale to ask the price of the house, and to get the key that he might look over it.

The price was so low that Yi Chang was startled. 'Why, the owner must be mad!' he said.

'Well, you see,' said the official, 'it's only fair to tell you that the house has been empty for a very long time, because it's said to be haunted. Of course it's all nonsense – a creak of the old timbers in the night, or the moon shining through a dusty window, and, there you are, the place gets a bad name.'

'Well, I'm not afraid of creaks in the night,' said Yi Chang. 'And as to dusty windows – a mop and a pail of water will soon remedy that!'

And then and there he bought the house, and fetched his two brothers, Hu and Ho, to come and help him clean up.

The house was handsomely furnished; but there was dust and there were spiders' webs everywhere. With brooms and mops and scrubbing brushes, the three young fellows worked all day. The paper walls were intact, and the sliding doors opened easily. By evening they had every room cleaned but one; and that one they couldn't get into, because the door of it was fast locked and there was no key.

'I wonder what's in there!' said Yi Chang. 'May as well have a look.'

And he took his knife from his girdle, slit a little hole in the paper wall and peeped through.

What did he see? A very big bare room. And on the floor of the room, a harp with broken strings, a pair of worn out shoes, and an old kettle.

Then Hu and Ho had a peep through the door.

'Nobody in their right mind would go and lock up such trash as that!' said Hu.

'Best break into the room and burn the rubbish!' said Ho.

'No, no,' said Yi Chang. 'I think *somebody* has put the things there. And maybe to that somebody they are precious. We'll leave them lie. . . . And I think it's time we stopped work,' said he, 'and had a bite to eat. The sun has set already, but the evening is warm. Let us go out on to the verandah and watch for the moon to rise.'

So they went out on to the verandah, and there they saw something they hadn't expected to see. At each end of the verandah lay a huge dog. One dog was yellow brown, the other was black as night.

'Now how did they get here?' said Hu. And he strolled up to the yellow brown dog and stroked it gently.

The dog didn't move.

'Is it alive?' said Yi Chang.

Hu nodded.

He went to the black dog and stroked it gently.

'This one is alive too,' he said.

'Well, we'll let them be,' said Yi Chang. 'They're doing no harm.'

Then the three brothers sat down on the verandah floor, and ate and drank the food and wine they had brought with them.

And they were tired. They didn't watch for the moon to rise. After they had eaten, they lay down on the verandah floor and fell asleep.

All quiet: not a breath of wind, not a rustle of the trees down below in the garden. Yi Chang was dreaming – well what was he dreaming? Of dogs and brooms and scrubbing brushes and pockets full of gold, all mixed up, when he was suddenly wakened by a hurried *tip-tap tip-tap* of the dogs' feet on the tiled floor of the verandah.

Yi Chang sat up, looked about him. The moon was rising in a cloudless sky, and everything was clear to see: the huddled figures of his two sleeping brothers, and the excited running to and fro of the dogs.

Then from somewhere in the town a gong struck the hour. It was midnight. And at the same moment the dogs set up a loud baying. Hu and Ho woke and scrambled to their feet. They were terrified, they were making a dash to get out of the verandah and back into the house when Yi Chang caught hold of them, one by each arm.

'Dumb heads!' he whispered. 'What are you afraid of? Just two dogs baying the moon! See, they are not taking the least notice of us. Come here into the shadow and watch.'

Now Hu and Ho felt rather ashamed of themselves. They drew back with Yi Chang into a corner of the verandah that was not lit by the moon.

And all of a sudden the baying of the dogs changed into a clear joyous barking. Now they were up on their hind legs, wagging their tails; and there in the middle of the verandah stood a little old gentleman, dressed in an elegant white silk robe with flowing sleeves. He had a high white hat on his head, and he was smoking a pipe; and as he leaned forward to caress the dogs, he seemed to be appearing and disappearing, one moment as solid as everything round him, the next moment a mere shadow.

So, having stroked the dogs with his long white hand, the little old gentleman moved with stately steps along the verandah, passed through a closed window as if it had been just so much air, and disappeared into the house.

'I'm not letting him out of my sight,' whispered Yi Chang, and he ran to the window, pulled it open and scrambled through with Hu and Ho at his heels – for they weren't going to be left behind on the verandah, where they felt that at any moment some other spectral figures might appear.

The moon was shining in through all the windows, making pools of light on the floors, and brightening the hangings on the walls. But the corners of the rooms, and all the passages, were in darkness. The white-robed little gentleman was nowhere to be seen. Only from somewhere ahead of them the brothers could hear the sound of music, and a very light *tip-a-tap* of dancing feet.

'This way!' whispered Yi Chang. Hurrying on, followed by his two brothers, and with the sound of the music and the dancing feet growing ever louder and louder, he came at last to the locked room.

Yi Chang peeped through the hole in the wall: the hole which you will remember he had made earlier in the day with his knife.

And what did he see now? A great company of gaily dressed Spectres whirling round in the gayest, maddest, jauntiest dance. A very old Spectre with a long white beard was sitting on the upturned kettle playing the harp, whose strings were not now broken, but in perfect order; and at his feet sat two smaller Spectres, one playing the fiddle, one beating the drum.

'Well, if this isn't delightful!' thought Yi Chang. And he stepped away from the door, and whispered to his brothers to take a peep.

Hu was just about to put his eye to the hole when he jumped back – and only just in time, for thrusting through the hole came a blue sword blade that shone with a dazzling light.

Hu gave a muffled shriek and fled back through the house. He didn't stop running until he was out on the verandah, where the high-risen moon shone down on the shaggy bodies of the sleeping dogs. Ho fled after him; and Yi Chang, wondering if he might take another peep through the hole, and deciding that the Spectres didn't want to be looked at, followed slowly.

'After all,' he said to himself, 'who am I that I should spy upon them?'

So he curled up on the verandah and went to sleep. And Hu slept and Ho slept, and the dogs slept. And the moon moved over the sky from the east, and went down in the west; and the sun rose in the east, and shone into the faces of the sleepers, and woke them. They scrambled to their feet, and looked about them. There were just the three of them on the verandah: the dogs had gone.

'Brother Chang,' said Hu, 'we must break our way into that room. And whatever we find there we must destroy. For it is well known that the way to drive off such uncanny visitors as Spectres is to burn everything they make use of.'

'That seems hard on them,' said Yi Chang. 'I wouldn't like it myself. But of course if it's only a matter of a harp with broken strings, a pair of worn out shoes, and an old kettle (which is all we saw there when we first looked into the room) – well, perhaps such rubbish is best out of the way. If the Spectres come again, they may be pleased to find the room tidied up.'

So the three brothers went to the locked room and broke through the paper wall. The room was just as they had first seen it yesterday: there was nothing in it but the harp with the broken strings, the pair of worn out shoes, and the rusty kettle. These things they carried out into the back garden. And there they heaped up a pile of dry leaves and twigs, and set the pile alight.

When the fire was burning brightly, Hu flung the old worn out pair of shoes into the flames, and Ho threw the kettle into the flames, and Yi Chang threw the harp into the flames. But scarcely had he done so than he seemed to hear a voice crying out, 'No, no!' And he made a snatch, heedless of the pain it gave him, and dragged all three things out of the fire.

Now there he was, flinging earth on the fire, and trampling it out with his feet.

'Stop! Stop! Have you gone mad?' shouted Hu. 'Don't you understand that we are doing the only thing possible to free the house from unwanted Spectres?'

'Brother Hu,' answered Yi Chang, 'I think the house belongs to *them* (whoever they may be) just as much as it belongs to me. And assuredly the kettle and the shoes and the harp are not mine, but theirs. Who am I that I should destroy what is theirs? No, no, we must put these things back where we found them.'

'And join in the devilish revels of their owners, I suppose?' sneered Ho.

'If they asked us, it would be only courteous to do so,' answered Yi Chang.

'Well, all I can say is that I'm not stopping here another night!' said Ho.

'Nor am I,' said Hu.

And then and there they turned their backs on Yi Chang, and went off to their house in the country.

But they weren't happy. They kept thinking of Yi Chang, living all alone in that haunted house – if, indeed, he were still alive.

'Oh, brother Ho,' said Hu, 'what if those Spectres have fallen on our poor Yi Chang and torn him limb from limb? I cannot sleep at night for thinking of him! I think we must go back and see what has become of him.'

'Yes,' said Ho, 'let us go.'

So they set out. They had a long journey, and didn't arrive at the house until just on midnight. It was a night of full moon again, and as they stood, gazing up at the house, and wondering if they dare venture in, a gong in the town struck twelve. Then they heard the joyous barking of the dogs. Immediately every window in the house was lighted up, and a sound of merry music floated out into the night. And not only merry music, but laughter and the sound of dancing feet.

'Oh, my poor brother Yi Chang!' whispered Hu. 'To think of him in there!'

'If he is still alive,' whispered Ho. 'Come, we must not stand here like cowards, we *must* venture in!'

Trembling, fearing they knew not what, they opened the gate. And as they stood there, trying to make up their minds to go up to the house door, that door was suddenly flung open, and there was Yi Chang running down the garden path towards them.

'Welcome, welcome, dear brothers!' cried Yi Chang. 'Come in and meet my friends!'

'Your *friends*!' exclaimed Hu. 'Have you really made friends with those – those – oh, are you not afraid of them?'

'Of course I'm not,' said Yi Chang. 'Why should I fear my friends?'

'But – but – ' whispered Ho, 'who are they? And – and *what* are they?'

Yi Chang shrugged his shoulders. 'I don't know exactly who or what they are,' he said. 'What does it matter? They are the happiest, merriest company ever you could meet with. We dance until we are tired of dancing, and then we sit to refresh ourselves with such wine and such delicacies as *you*, my brothers, have never yet tasted. And they tell such wonderful, wonderful stories; and the time goes by like the swift flight of a beautiful bird. But why do we stand here? Come – the music calls us!'

But Hu and Ho couldn't be persuaded to set foot in that house. They made excuses. They said that they were on a business journey, and must hurry. They said they had only just paused in passing to assure themselves that Yi Chang was well and happy.

Yi Chang laughed: he saw through all their excuses. But he embraced them both in brotherly fashion, and went back into the house.

Shutting the gate carefully behind them, Hu and Ho walked on their way, back towards their home. They walked for a long time in silence.

Then Hu said, 'Our brother Yi Chang is certainly a very friendly person.'

'Yes,' agreed Ho. He paused and then said, 'I think it is good to be friendly.'

'Even with Spectres?' said Hu.

'Better friends than enemies with those fellows,' said Ho.

7 · *Dilly-dilly-doh!*

One Christmas Eve, a young girl sat in a farm kitchen, rocking a baby to sleep. It was very quiet in the farm, because everyone else, the farmer and his wife, and their sons and daughters, and the rest of the servants, had gone to Midnight Mass in the church across the hills. But of course someone had to stay and mind the baby, whose name was Kari. So there the young girl sat, and rocked the cradle. And as she rocked she sang:

> '*Sleep, little Kari dear,*
> *Naught shall come to harm you here,*
> Lully-lully-loh!'

Then Something came to stand and listen outside the window. And that Something was *A GREAT BIG SPOOK.*

The Spook bent down, peered in through the window and said:

> '*Sweet sounds your song to me,*
> *Wild and wailing mine must be,*
> Dilly-dilly-doh!'

And the girl answered:

> '*Wild words I will not hear,*
> *Sleep, little Kari dear,*
> Lully-lully-loh!'

Then the Spook spoke again:

'Soft seem your hands to me,
Gnarled and twisted mine must be,
Dilly-dilly-doh!'

And the girl answered:

'Dirt my hands shall never sweep,
Sleep, little Kari, sleep,
Lully-lully-loh!'

Then the Spook said:

'Fair seem your eyes to me,
Huge and staring mine must be,
Dilly-dilly-doh!'

And the girl answered:

'My eyes shall not look on ill.
Sleep Kari, lie you still,
Lully-lully-loh!'

Then the Spook said:

'Dainty seem your feet to me,
Big and clumping mine must be,
Dilly-dilly-doh!'

And the girl answered:

'Dirt shall never touch my feet.
Hush, my Kari, hush, my sweet,
Lully-lully-loh!'

Then the Spook cried:

'Dawn in the East I see!
Rough, ah rough, the road for me!
Dilly-dilly-doh!'

And the girl answered:

> *'Christmas Day has now begun.*
> *Stand out there and turn to stone!*
> *Hush, Kari, hush, my own,*
> Lully-lully-loh!'

Then with a long wailing cry the Spook went away from the window.

And in the morning, when the farm folk came home, they found a huge grey stone standing in the courtyard.

And it stands there to this day.

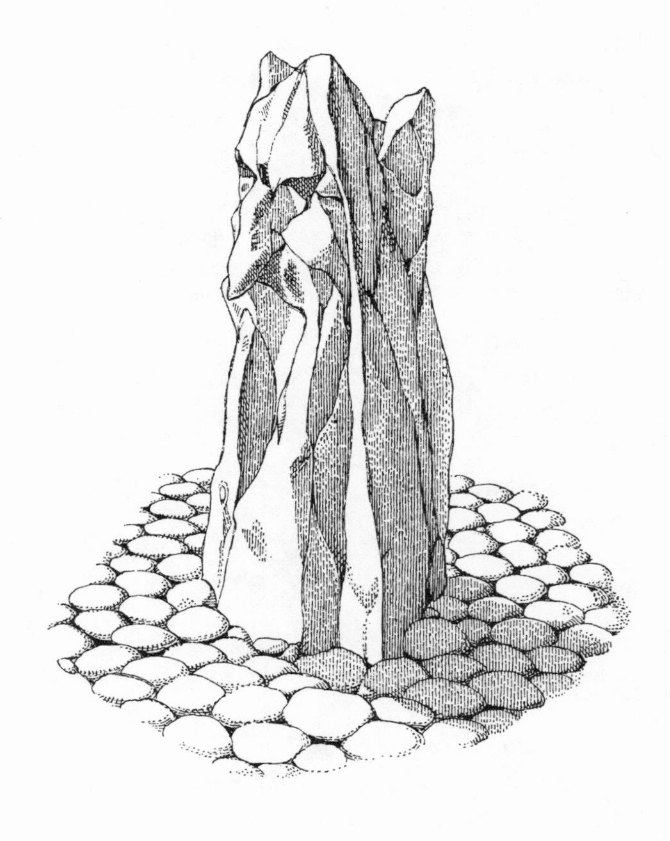

8 · The Owl

Once upon a time there was a man called Josep who lived in a small house up among the mountains. Josep had ten goats, four cows, an old sow and seven little piglings. By day he pastured these animals in one or other of the mountain meadows. But by night, to keep them safe from marauding wolves and wandering night spirits, he housed them all: the goats in the barn, the cows in the byre, and the sow and the seven piglings in their sty.

And not until he had seen all these animals safely housed did Josep go into his kitchen to get his supper.

Well now, one beautiful summer evening, Josep, having seen to the bedding of his animals, was just about to go into his little house. He was feeling happy, he was humming a tune, when he heard a loud screech, *To-whit, to-whoo-oo-oo*! And looking up, he saw a big owl perched on the lintel of the porch door.

It was a *very* big owl, and when it saw Josep it screeched all the louder. So Josep laughed and sang out:

> *'Owl, owl, you foolish old fowl,*
> *Why sit there making a din?*
> *If you're lacking in meat,*
> *And wishful to eat,*
> *To my kitchen I beg you step in, step in,*
> *To my kitchen I beg you step in!'*

Well, of course Josep didn't really expect the owl to step into his kitchen. He was just making fun of it. So he was absolutely astounded when – after he had gone in and shut the door, and was busy at the kitchen fire, cooking his evening meal of cheese and macaroni – the door was suddenly flung open and in strode a *huge great man*. The size of the man was in itself alarming. But what was really terrifying was that *the man had an owl's head*. In fact, he was a Spook.

And the huge great man with the owl's head roared out in a huge great voice: 'YOU INVITED ME. I HAVE COME. WHAT WILL YOU GIVE ME TO EAT?'

Was Josep scared? He was! All alone among the mountains with a Spook, and not a neighbour within miles! 'Oh sir,' he stammered, 'I didn't – didn't expect – but if you wish for food there is a bowl of milk here, and – and some macaroni in the pan on the fire.'

Owl Head seized the bowl of milk. One gulp – the bowl was empty. He snatched the pan off the fire – another gulp: pan and all had gone down his throat. And he roared out again: 'I AM HUNGRY. WHAT WILL YOU GIVE ME TO EAT?'

'I – I have two cheeses on the shelf there,' said Josep.

Owl Head took the cheeses off the shelf. *Gulp*, he swallowed one cheese. *Gulp*, he swallowed the other cheese. And now he was roaring out again: 'I AM HUNGRY. GIVE ME TO EAT!'

'Open the cupboard then if you must,' cried Josep. 'Eat everything you find there: the bread, the flour, the salt, the sugar, the coffee, the rice – '

Owl Head gave such a tug at the cupboard door that the door came off in his hand. One moment the cupboard was full of food; next moment it was empty. Everything in it, bread, flour, salt, sugar, coffee, rice, had gone down the monster's throat. And he whizzed round to face Josep, and again roared out: 'I AM HUNGRY. WHAT WILL YOU GIVE ME TO EAT?'

'Here is the – the key of the dairy,' stammered Josep. 'You – you will find a tub of milk there, and – and some cheeses and butter on the dairy shelf.'

Spook Owl Head seized the key and went into the dairy. Five minutes later he came back into the kitchen. 'The dairy is now bare,' he howled. 'And I am hungry – give me to eat.'

'I have nothing more,' said Josep.

'You have cows in the byre, you have goats in the barn, you have a sow and her piglings in the sty,' roared the monster. 'And I AM HUNGRY. I MUST EAT!'

'Oh no! Oh no!' cried Josep.

But the Spook Owl Head had rushed out of the house. Now he was in the sty, swallowing pig and piglings, now he was in the barn, gobbling up the goats. Now he was in the byre, cramming one cow after another down his great throat. But when he was about to snatch up the last cow, he gave a shriek and ran out of the byre. For that cow had a bell hung round her neck, and on the bell was a picture of the Madonna.

Next moment Owl Head was back in the kitchen again, and again he was roaring out that he was hungry and must have something to eat.

'I have nothing more to give you,' said Josep.

'*What! Nothing more!*' bellowed Owl Head. 'Then I will eat *you*!'

Now on the window-sill in the kitchen was a Bible which Josep sometimes, but not very often, read on Sunday afternoons when he had nothing else to do. Now, in his desperation, he snatched up that Bible, and clasping it against his breast, he cried out: 'The dear God, and Christ the Lord, and all His saints defend me!'

When the Spook heard those words, flames flew from his mouth, and fiery sparkles from his eyes. He gave one shriek, and rushed out of the house.

And in his terror Josep fell to the floor in a faint. . . .

When he came to himself, he found the milk back in the bowl, the macaroni back in the pan, all the food back in the cupboard, the milk, the cheeses, and the butter back in the dairy, the pig and her piglings back in the sty, the goats back in the barn, and all the cows back in the byre.

But from that day to the end of his life, never did Josep dare to make fun of any living creature, whether bird or beast or even insect, lest that creature should turn out to be a Spook.

9 · *The Black Spectre*

A merchant had three sons. We needn't bother about the names of two of them, but the youngest was called Jack. Jack was a simple lad. His two brothers looked down on him, and thought him a fool. However, Jack was anything but a fool, as you will agree when you have read this story.

Well now, Jack's two brothers had a mind to travel and see the world; and their father was quite willing that they should go. So they set out, each with plenty of money in his pocket, and each with a fine horse to ride.

Yes, they set out, but they didn't come back. And that worried Jack. 'Father,' said he, 'where *are* my brothers?'

'Enjoying themselves in some place or other, I suppose,' said his father.

'Then what about me?' said Jack. 'Why shouldn't I also be enjoying myself in some place or other?'

'Because I think you are better at home,' said his father.

'But I too should like to see something of the world,' said Jack. And he said this so often that at last his father answered, 'Oh, very well.' Then he gave Jack a good little horse and a purse full of money. And Jack set out.

Away he rode, and on he rode. He saw towns and villages, and people working in the fields, and people trudging along the roads, and people driving to market, and people buying and selling in the markets. But he saw nothing very different from anything he might have seen at home.

'If this is the world,' said Jack to himself, 'I don't think much of it!'

Well, one early evening, when he was on the look out for

somewhere to spend the night, he came to a roadside tavern. On the opposite side of the road was a little hill, and near the top of the little hill was a castle. You couldn't call the castle a ruin, because all its walls stood up stout and strong; but it had an empty, dreary look, as though no one had lived in it for a very long time.

Jack gave a glance up at the castle; and then he went into the tavern.

'Hey, landlord, can you give me some supper and a bed for the night? And have you a good stable and fodder for my little horse?'

The landlord said he could and he had. So Jack jumped off his horse and went with the landlord to the stable.

But when the landlord opened the stable door, Jack got a surprise. What did he see, each in a stall and munching oats, but his brothers' two horses!

'Oh, oh, landlord, where did you get those two horses? Did you buy them in the market, and are you thinking to sell them?'

'Nay,' said the landlord, 'I neither bought them, nor do I mean to sell them. They belong to two young gentlemen. And I wish those two gentlemen would come and fetch them, that I do! But I fear me they never will.'

'And where are those two gentlemen, landlord?'

'Well, sir, they went up to the castle yonder, and they didn't come back. It's a sad case, sir, nobody who goes up to that castle ever does come back.'

'I must look into this,' thought Jack. And he didn't even wait to have his supper. He just stayed long enough to see his little horse fed, watered and bedded down, and then off with him up to the castle, with the landlord standing at the door of the tavern, and shouting after him not to go.

But Jack would go. He climbed up the little hill, came to the castle, found the great entrance door unlocked, pushed it open, and went in.

The castle was finely furnished, and all the rooms were in spick and span order; but he didn't find his brothers there. In fact, he didn't find anybody, and though he shouted himself hoarse, he got no answer. So he went out again, and stood looking out over one of the rampart walls, wondering what he should do next.

On the wall there was an elder bush, covered with ripe berries.

'Those berries would make a nice pudding,' thought Jack. And he picked a hatful.

Now it was growing dark, so he went back into the castle. He was still thinking of his brothers, and he didn't mean to leave the place until he got some tidings of them; or at least could assure himself that they had been there and gone.

So, wandering from room to room, he came into the castle kitchen, where there was a stack of firewood. He piled wood on the hearth, took out his tinder box, and lit a fire. Then he rummaged in the kitchen cupboards, found flour and sugar, and set about making an elderberry pudding. He felt very proud of himself when he had that pudding tied up in a cloth and hanging in a crock of boiling water over the fire. He was licking his lips and thinking what a good meal he would have very soon, when the kitchen door opened and Some One came in. Well, did you ever? That Some One was an old Black Spectre. And the Black Spectre was scowling.

'Ha!' said Jack. 'Good evening to you! I'm glad you've come, because truth to tell I was beginning to feel lonely. Now you shall share my pudding. But you must wait a while, because it isn't cooked yet.'

'I WILL *NOT* WAIT,' snarled the Black Spectre. 'You must come with me *at once*!'

'Oh no,' said Jack, 'I can't come with you anywhere just now. Because, you see, my pudding might burn.'

'If you don't come at once,' snarled the Black Spectre, 'I WILL TEAR YOU UP.'

'What, you old ink blot!' said Jack. '*You* threaten to tear *me* up? That settles it. I'm not going a single step with you.'

The Black Spectre changed his tune then. He began to whimper. 'I want you to come, oh, I do want you to come! And the pudding *won't* be burned, I give you my word. Oh, dear me, do come, *do* come!'

And now there was actually a tear trickling down that old spectre's black cheek.

Jack didn't like to see that tear, so he said, 'Oh, very well, I'll come. But understand, old fellow, if my pudding *does* burn, I'll never forgive you!'

'It will *not* burn,' said the spectre again. And he led the way out of the kitchen and down some stairs, with Jack following.

At the bottom of the stairs they came to a closed door.

'Open it,' said the Black Spectre.

'Now see here,' said Jack, 'I don't take kindly to being ordered about by the likes of you. If you want the door opened, you can open it yourself.'

The Black Spectre gave a little moan. But he opened the door; and they went through into a big room.

In the room was a huge dog, with sparks coming out of his eyes, and flames coming out of his mouth. And the huge dog made a rush at Jack. But Jack gave a blow with his fist and a kick with his foot, and the huge dog ran off up the stairs, howling, with the sparks flying out of him on every side.

Jack watched him and laughed. Then he remembered his pudding. And he turned to follow the dog up the stairs. But the Black Spectre had crossed the room to another door, which had a great bar across it. And he was calling on Jack to unbar the door and open it.

'Why should I?' said Jack. 'If you opened one door, you can open another. I must go back to the kitchen. Even as I stand here, that great lump of a dog may be gobbling up my pudding.'

'The dog can't gobble it up,' wailed the Black Spectre. 'He can't even reach it, and besides it will be much too hot. Oh do, *do* open the door!'

'No, I won't open it, and that's flat,' said Jack.

So then the Black Spectre unbarred the door himself. And Jack, after thinking this way and that way for a moment, decided that the Black Spectre was right about the safety of the pudding. So he followed the spectre into another big room.

This room was full of snakes, writhing and hissing and darting out their forked tongues. The Black Spectre picked up a whip that was lying on the floor. He handed the whip to Jack and said, 'Chase the creatures out.'

'Not I!' said Jack. 'They'll only go upstairs and eat my pudding.'

'They won't, they can't, they don't want to,' moaned the Black Spectre. 'Whoever heard of snakes eating elderberry pudding? Oh do, *do* drive them out!'

'Oh well,' said Jack, 'perhaps you're right. Perhaps snakes don't eat puddings. So, just to oblige you, old fellow, though there's no sense in it . . . '

Then he whisked the whip this way and that way over the heads of the snakes. And the snakes fled from the room, scrambling over each other in their haste to get away.

Meanwhile the Black Spectre had crossed the room to yet another door, and he was calling on Jack to open it.

'No, I'm not coming a step farther with you,' said Jack. 'Though that brute of a dog mayn't be able to reach my pudding, and though the snakes mayn't want to eat it, how do I know that the water under it hasn't boiled dry? How do I know that my pudding isn't getting burned to a cinder at this moment?'

'It isn't getting burnt, and it won't get burnt,' wailed the Black Spectre. 'Oh do, do open this last door, and I'll never ask you to do anything for me again! Surely you won't refuse an old fellow his last, his very last request?'

Now there were bright tears glittering in the Black Spectre's eyes, and one big tear was actually trickling down his cheek. So then Jack felt sorry for him, and opened the door.

Well, what a revolting sight! Three huge barrels stood on the floor, and the barrels were full of rats, bats, toads, and some creatures that Jack had never seen before: creatures that looked like little dragons. And all these creatures were hissing and squealing and shrieking and croaking.

'If this is your idea of a pretty picture, it isn't mine!' said Jack to the Black Spectre.

'Upset the barrels and turn the creatures out,' said the Black Spectre. 'And that is something I'm asking you to do for yourself, and not for me.'

'Oh well," said Jack, 'I don't suppose it matters now what I do. My pudding must certainly be burnt by this time. So here goes!'

And he took a run at the barrels, and turned them topsy-turvy, one after the other.

Hissing, squealing, croaking and shrieking all the creatures tumbled to the floor and rushed out of the room. The barrels swayed for a moment this way and that way. And then they stood upright again.

'That's odd!' said Jack. 'It's just as if the barrels had life in them.'

'They have *something* in them,' said the Black Spectre. 'And though it isn't life, it's something that makes life pleasant. Take a look, Jack.'

Jack looked into the barrels. Oh ho! Oh ho! The barrels were full to the brim with money. In the first barrel there were copper coins, in the second barrel were silver coins, in the third barrel were gold coins.

'Jack-Without-Fear – for so I must henceforth call you,' said the Black Spectre, 'all this money is yours, to do with what you will. But take my advice, Jack. Give the copper coins to the poor, give the silver coins to the church, and keep the gold coins for yourself and for your father and your brothers. This castle too, which once was mine, is also yours. No, you needn't thank me. In my life I was a miserable old miser, Jack; I hoarded all this money, giving alms to none, and starving myself that I might add coin to coin. And so, when death came, Heaven's gates were shut against me, and I was doomed to wander miserably amongst my ill-gotten gains. But you have freed me, Jack-Without-Fear, and now I can go to my rest in the world of worlds.'

Whilst he so spoke the Black Spectre was all the time growing paler and paler. Now he was no longer a Black Spectre, but a White Spectre. And now that White Spectre was but a faint, faint Shadow. And now it altogether vanished.

'Well, I'll be blowed!' said Jack. 'What an old rascal! But if my pudding's burnt I'll never forgive him!'

And so saying, he turned and hurried back to the kitchen.

No, the pudding wasn't burnt. It was just nicely cooked. Jack ate it all. And then he lay down on the kitchen floor, yawned once, yawned twice, and fell asleep.

In the morning he left the castle and hurried down to the inn. The landlord was rejoiced to see him. 'For I feared you wasn't never coming back no more, sir, indeed I did,' said the landlord. 'Nobody never has come back no more that goes up to that cursed castle.'

'It isn't cursed any longer,' said Jack. 'And if I can only find my two brothers, all will end happily.'

And all did end happily. Jack gave the landlord some gold coins, jumped on his horse, and galloped home. And at home he found his two brothers, who had a sorrowful story to tell.

Yes, they had been to the castle, and had been so terrified by the Black Spectre that they had fled out by a back way, and hurried home across the hills, not even daring to go down to the inn for their horses.

When Jack told them *his* story they were amazed.

'You are a braver fellow than either of us,' said the eldest brother.

'Yes, and a better fellow,' said the second brother. 'And if we have ever mocked at you, Jack, and thought you a silly, you must forgive us.'

Of course Jack laughed, and said there was nothing to forgive. And he said too that his father and his brothers must now come to live with him in his castle, which they did.

And in that castle they lived happily ever after, seeing nothing of the Huge Dog, or of the Snakes, or of the other nasty creatures; for all these had vanished from the castle when the Black Spectre went to his rest in the World of Worlds.

10 · *Rubizal and the Miller's Daughter*

1. *What happened to Ludomilla's suitors*

The great and powerful Spook Rubizal lived on the mountains. The mountains belonged to Rubizal, and Rubizal belonged to the mountains. Everyone knew about him, but few people had seen him. In fact, few people desired to see him, because his power was very great; and though he was known to reward good people, he was also known to punish people who were not so good. And since we all have some little secret peccadillos on our conscience – well, there you are – on the whole it was better to keep out of Rubizal's way.

Now down in the valley under the mountain there lived a rich miller, a widower with one lovely daughter, called Ludomilla. Ludomilla was as good as she was beautiful, and since it was known that the miller had made a will, leaving all he possessed to Ludomilla, the girl had many suitors. Noblemen's sons, gentlemen's sons, farmers' sons, they all paid court to Ludomilla; and every evening the miller's parlour would be crowded with these young fellows, making free of the miller's wine, and casting languishing looks at the lovely Ludomilla, as she moved among them like some gracious goddess, filling their glasses, and handing round the cakes which her own fair hands had prepared and baked.

Ludomilla's father, the miller, delighted in these social gatherings, but Ludomilla herself disliked them intensely. 'Am I never to have any peace?' thought the poor girl. 'I don't care one pin for any of these lads – and why must I be pestered by them?'

Well, there came a day in autumn when Ludomilla felt she could bear this state of things no longer. And she put on her cape, drew the hood of the cape over her golden hair, and betook herself to the mountains to seek the help of Rubizal.

She had a hard climb before she reached the little plateau among the mountains that was known as Rubizal's Dell. And she was out of breath, and feeling more than a little scared. There she stood, all alone, and round her was silence. Dared she call that great spirit to her aid? . . . Yes, she dared, and she *must*, she told herself – why else had she come here?

'Rubizal,' she called in a little frightened voice. 'Oh great lord and master of the mountains, I, a poor unhappy maiden, beseech you to help me!'

And no sooner had she spoken these words than there was Rubizal standing before her: tall, majestic, with great flashing eyes, and hair that glittered in the sun, now gold, now ruddy, now darkly sparkling.

'You called me,' said Rubizal, in a voice that echoed among the mountains. 'And why have you called me?'

Then Ludomilla, at first falteringly, but gaining courage as she went along, told Rubizal of her troubles: all about her life and about her pestering suitors, and how her father would have her make her choice among them, and how she hated them – yes, *hated* them every one; and how she often thought she would run away from home, but then it would be cruel of her to desert her father – and oh, what was she to do, what *was* she to do?

Rubizal listened without saying a word. But when she had said her say, and was mopping up her eyes (for her story sounded very pathetic even in her own ears) Rubizal laid a hand, light as the brush of a bird's wing, on her shoulder, and said, 'Get you home now, Ludomilla. You shall be no more troubled. And not only shall you be no more troubled, but I will send you the desire of your heart. You don't know what *is* the desire of your heart? Ah, but Rubizal knows, my gentle little Ludomilla. Yes, Rubizal knows.'

So then Ludomilla made Rubizal a deep curtsy, and went home feeling much happier. 'My lord Rubizal will keep his word,' she was saying to herself. 'Oh yes, my lord Rubizal will keep his word. But that was a strange saying of his about *sending* me the desire of my heart! For surely the desire of my heart is only to be left in peace!'

Which just shows you how little the girl knew about herself.

That day some very strange things happened. And in the evening not a single suitor came to the mill. This annoyed the miller very much; but Ludomilla, after she had prepared her father's supper, went up to her room and sang in the lightness of her heart. She felt that a great burden had been lifted from her.

And what were the strange things that had been happening that day? To tell of them all would take too long, but I will give you an account of one or two of them.

Lawyer Clemens, who was one of the most ardent of the suitors, set out as usual in the early evening to visit the mill. Of course, as he had travelled the road to the mill so often, he knew every inch of the way. But he was somewhat startled when, as he was passing some bushes, he saw, rising from behind them, a clear blue flame.

'That is curious,' he said to himself, 'I don't remember seeing those bushes before. But if they have caught fire, it were well to put the fire out, before it does more damage.'

And he was hurrying to the bushes, when an ice-cold hand seized him by the shoulder. The ice-cold hand dragged him behind the bushes, it brought him to a well of ice-cold water, it plunged him into the ice-cold water once, twice, three times, it cast him out among the bushes. And as he fell among them, a voice roared in his ear, 'GO HOME!'

And home he went, shaking and shuddering, and now lay in bed with a fever.

So that was one suitor disposed of.

Another suitor was a neighbouring farmer's son; and he also set out that evening all cock-a-hoop to the mill. And what was his joyful surprise when, as he was half way to the mill, he saw Ludomilla coming to meet him. Yes, the bashful Ludomilla actually hurrying towards him, holding out both her hands, and smiling!

'So I am the chosen one, I am the lucky one!' thought the delighted farmer's son. 'A smack in the eye for your gentlemen!' And he ran to Ludomilla and took her in his arms.

Oh horror! It was not Ludomilla that he held in his arms, but a Gigantic Shape, that hugged him to its breast so tightly that he fainted. So that was another suitor disposed of.

But perhaps strangest of all was what happened to the rich young lord, Heinrich, who lived some distance from the mill on the other side of a forest. Lord Heinrich was the most favoured of all the suitors by the miller, because, though the miller was not grasping about money, it *would* be a fine thing to be able to speak to his cronies (in oh, such a careless tone) of 'my son-in-law Lord Heinrich.' But Ludomilla disliked the young lord intensely, not for himself, poor fellow, but because her father would keep dinning his name into her ears, telling her what a foolish girl she was to turn her back on him.

Well now, on this day of strange happenings, young Lord Heinrich set out as usual to visit the miller. In his pocket he had a present for Ludomilla, a pretty gold bracelet on which twinkled some truly magnificent diamonds. He would much rather have been bringing her a ring. For 'by my troth!' he thought, 'if I could but slip a ring on to her finger, and claim her as my future bride!' But the time had not come for that – and perhaps she would not even accept the bracelet! In that case he would feel like dashing out his brains!

It was with such thoughts, half hopeful, half despairing, that he was riding through the forest on his way to the mill, with a young page boy riding at a little distance behind him, when suddenly there came such a furious storm of wind rushing through the forest as set the horses back on their haunches, and flung both young Lord Heinrich and the page violently to the ground.

'Oh, master,' cried the page, as they both scrambled to their feet, 'this is an ill omen! We should turn back home before worse befalls us!'

'Turn back home indeed, you young fool!' exclaimed Lord Heinrich. 'Turn back for a blast of wind that even now has died

away! Get up in the saddle again, and follow me. And let me hear no more of your nonsense about ill omens!'

So they remounted, and rode on.

Well, they hadn't ridden much farther when again there came that furious storm of wind. It rushed through the forest with a roaring and a crashing of branches; and to his horror the young page saw Lord Heinrich snatched off his horse and whirled up into the air.

Up, up, above the tops of the highest trees, went Lord Heinrich, whirling round and round, and being carried, not in the direction of the mill, but back in the direction of his own castle.

At the same time the young page was again flung from his horse. Now both the horses kicked up their heels and galloped away. And the young page set off running towards home, ever seeing in front of him Lord Heinrich, tossing and whirling above the forest trees, like any boy's kite being blown by a strong wind.

Now the page came once more in sight of Lord Heinrich's castle. But where was Lord Heinrich? Had the demons of the air carried him away to some terrible den of their own, never to be seen again by mortal eyes? Panting for breath, the young page stood gazing round him. Then he heard a feeble cry for help. And in a quarry by the roadside he saw Lord Heinrich, his master, lying bruised and battered and scarcely conscious.

So the page lifted Lord Heinrich on to his shoulders, and carried him home.

Truly Rubizal had his own merry notions of the way to dispose of Ludomilla's suitors! It would take too long to tell of all the crazy tricks he played. Enough to say that on that evening not one of these suitors arrived at the mill. Nor did any suitors come to the mill on the next day, or on any following day. Ludomilla sang as she went about her work, and blessed Rubizal in her heart. But the miller was sorely vexed. He couldn't understand it, and it irked him to spend his evenings with a few elderly neighbours, who were the only people that Rubizal allowed to visit the mill.

2. *Ludomilla Finds her True Lover*

Some weeks after these stirring events, a young lad called Larry was crossing the mountains in search of work. Larry's mother had died when he was a little boy; and just lately his father, who was a miller like Ludomilla's father, had gone bankrupt and died. Now there was nothing for Larry to do but to sell the mill to pay his father's debts, and to go out into the world to seek for work.

But so far he had not been successful in finding work. Farmers wanted lads accustomed to horses; merchants wanted lads who were smart at handling money, and who understood the tricks of buying and selling; shopkeepers wanted lads who could wheedle folk into purchasing goods they really had no need of. Poor Larry was deficient in all these ways: he was just an honest lad willing to turn his hand to any work. But there – it seemed that nobody wanted him.

So it was in a somewhat dreary mood that Larry came over the crest of the mountains, and sat down to rest and look about him. And he hadn't sat there long when he saw, standing by his side, a tall, handsome gentleman with great flashing eyes and hair that glittered like gold in the rays of the sun.

'Good day, young fellow,' said the tall handsome gentleman.

'Good day to you, sir,' said Larry.

'Out seeking for work?' said the tall handsome gentleman.

'Just so, sir,' said Larry.

'Any particular trade?' said the tall handsome gentleman.

'Well, sir,' said Larry, 'I shouldn't mind turning my hand to any kind of work. But I am a miller's son, and milling is the work I understand best.'

'Just so,' said the tall handsome gentleman. 'And as it happens there is a mill down yonder in the valley. It is possible, just possible, that the miller might give you employment.'

'I'll go down there at once,' said Larry. 'But – '

'Oh yes, yes, I know,' said the tall handsome gentleman. 'You are weary. Perhaps first a little rest, a little shutting of the eyes, a little doze . . .'

The tall handsome gentleman's hand was waving to and fro in front of Larry's eyes; the tall handsome gentleman's voice was becoming less and less distinct in Larry's ear. Larry's head nodded, his eyes closed: next moment he was fast asleep.

The tall handsome gentleman (who as you must have guessed, was none other than the Spook Rubizal) chuckled. He pointed a long forefinger in the direction of the mill, saw, with eyes that could see through most things, a thin curling spiral of smoke rising from the roof of the mill, took on himself the likeness of the sleeping Larry, and with a chuckling laugh went swiftly striding down the mountain.

And as he went, the thin spiral of smoke that was rising from the mill became a dense smoke. Bright flames followed the smoke, leaping from the roof, flashing and crackling. 'Fire! Fire! The mill is on fire! Bring water! Bring water!' People were shouting, people were rushing, everything was in confusion.

But see now, in the midst of the confusion, a lad whom no one knows has climbed up on to the roof. He is tearing away the smouldering beams and flinging them to the ground. With a loud commanding voice he is ordering the people to hand him up their buckets full of water, he is dashing the water on to the roof, he is tossing down the empty buckets, and calling on the people to hand him up more full buckets, and more, and these too he is emptying on to the flames. He has taken charge of everything, he seems to have no fear, and gradually, gradually the flames die down, die out, and though the wooden roof is badly burned, the mill itself is saved.

'Where is that lad, that gallant lad? Bring him to me that I may thank and reward him!' cries the miller.

But the gallant lad has disappeared: the people scurry round looking for him. No, no one can find him. The miller goes into his parlour, and flops down in an armchair, quite overcome; and his daughter Ludomilla, who is herself shuddering with the after effects of fear and excitement, pours him out a glass of brandy, and thinks of the gallant lad, wondering if she will ever see him again.

Meanwhile the gallant lad, who, as you must have guessed, was

no other than Rubizal himself, has gone back up the mountain. Now he is the tall handsome gentleman again, and the tall handsome gentleman is stooping over the sleeping Larry and shaking him.

'Wake up, young rascal, wake up!' Rubizal is saying. 'It is time you were going on your way!'

Larry sits up, rubs his eyes. 'I have had such a strange dream about the mill,' he says. 'I dreamed that it was on fire; and I dreamed I – oh what nonsense! I dreamed that I was up on the mill roof and that – that . . . '

'You were putting out the fire?' said the tall handsome gentleman. 'Well, well, it may be that others have had the same dream about you. Come, be off! I think you will find a welcome waiting for you down at the mill.'

So Larry got up and went his way down the mountain to the mill. And there indeed he *did* find a welcome! The people gathered round him, shouting and cheering. They brought him in to the miller, who leaped up from his chair and flung his arms round the astonished lad, thanking him with the tears streaming down his face.

'But – but I have done nothing!' stammered Larry.

'*Nothing!*' cried the miller. 'Oh, my dear good lad, what do I not owe you? What can I do for you? Anything, anything – only tell me!'

'If you could give me work,' said Larry. 'I . . . '

'Give you work!' cried the miller. 'Of course I will give you work if that is what you need! You shall live in my house, you shall be to me as a son, you shall – ' he glanced at Ludomilla. 'If you will you shall marry my daughter.'

Larry looked at Ludomilla. Ludomilla looked at Larry. Larry thought he had never seen a lovelier maiden; Ludomilla felt that she loved Larry with all her heart. As soon as it might be arranged, even before the mill roof was repaired, Ludomilla and Larry were married. And Larry settled down to a happy life, working with the miller.

Yes, a happy life, and yet Larry was troubled. And one day he said to Ludomilla, 'Dear wife, I feel that I do not deserve my good fortune. Whoever put out the fire, it was not I.'

And he told her all about his meeting with the tall handsome gentleman on the mountain, and of his falling asleep, and of his dream.

'It was only in a dream that I stood on the burning roof of the mill and put out the fire,' he said.

Ludomilla laughed. 'Then it was all Rubizal's doing,' she said. 'But why should you fret yourself? Rubizal has sent me a husband to love, and he has sent my father a son-in-law whom he admires and trusts. So what else matters?'

11 · The Spook and the Beer Barrel

Once upon a time five merry little Spooks were ambling about the world, arm in arm, just for the sake of adventure.

They were up to no end of mischief. They made themselves invisible, and when they found people about to sit down for a meal, they pulled the chairs from under them, and scampered off, squealing with laughter to see the people tumble down, *bump*, *bump*, *bump* on to the floor. They snatched off the hats of men they met walking in the streets and put the hats on their own heads, so that the astonished men saw their hats bobbing away down the streets with nothing under them. They followed pretty girls, jumped on their shoulders, tweaked their hair, and shouted 'Boo!' in their ears. They set dogs howling, and cats spitting, and pigs squealing. They leaped on to the backs of horses and set them madly galloping. And when they wearied of all this fun, they ran into rich Mr Berg's wine cellar to rest and refresh themselves.

There were bottles of wine and barrels of beer in the cellar. The Spooks took the corks out of the bottles and tasted the wine. They drew the bungs from the barrels and tasted the beer. On the whole they preferred the beer; and they became so merry that they were singing and dancing down there and making such a racket that Mr Berg came hurrying to see what all the noise was about.

There was a window in the cellar that opened into a yard, and four of the Spooks managed to scramble through the window and get away. But somehow the window got slammed behind them, and there was one little Spook left in the cellar, and dodging about among the beer barrels, looking for somewhere to hide. Then this little Spook saw an empty barrel with the bung lying beside it, and he crept in through the bung hole and curled up inside the barrel. But in his hurry he had forgotten to make himself invisible, and Mr Berg caught sight of him as he crept in. So what did Mr Berg do but push the bung back into the barrel, and go off laughing to tell his wife what he had done.

And there was the poor little Spook nicely trapped.

What to do? Well, he must somehow make a hole in the barrel big enough to creep through. And he set about making it with his sharp nails and sharper teeth. By morning he had a hole big enough to put his leg through. And he had just got one leg out of the hole when he heard Mr Berg coming down the stairs into the cellar. Then the little Spook took fright; and there he was, dodging past Mr Berg and up the cellar steps hopping on his one leg, with the rest of him still inside the barrel, and so hop, hop, hop, barrel and all, out into the yard, where the dogs were howling and running off with their tails between their legs, and Mr Berg giving chase, scarcely able to run for laughing, and yet angry too.

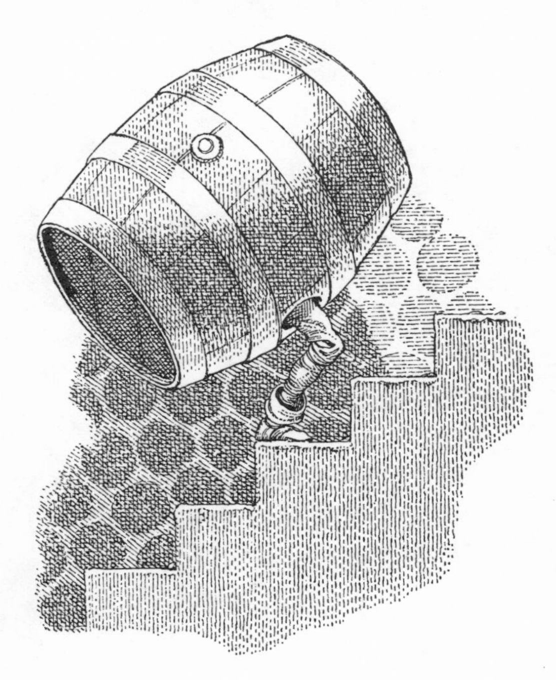

The barrel was heavy. The poor little Spook was puffing and panting and hardly able to hop another step on his one leg, when fortunately for him he crashed the barrel against the yard wall, and it fell to pieces. Now the little Spook was free, and he fled to join his comrades, whom he found in Mr Berg's orchard, pulling the apples off the trees. They stayed in the orchard all day; and that night they went back into the wine cellar, and pulled the bungs out of all the barrels – just to teach Mr Berg a lesson, so they said.

Then they scampered back to Spook Land.

And in the morning, when Mr Berg went down in to his cellar, he found the place a-swim with beer.

And that truly was very hard lines on Mr Berg, because after all it was his beer, and the Spooks had no business to meddle with it.

But, there you are, the Spooks never did know the difference between right and wrong.

12 · *Tummeldink*

Well, who and what was Tummeldink? As far as anyone knew he was a little ball of fire, that, on dark nights, burned like a bundle of straw, leaping this way, leaping that way. An alarming sight, one might think, for a benighted traveller to meet with when far from home. And so, at first, many a weary and benighted traveller did think. But by and by such a traveller not only ceased to fear that ball of fire, he welcomed it with delight. For whether that fire moved straight on, or whether it turned to the left or to the right, you had but to follow it, and it led you safely home.

Now Tummeldink hadn't always been a ball of fire. Once he had been a living man, a rich man and a proud one, who took pleasure in boasting of his riches, and of how he gave food and money to the poor. But when a poor man, with a heart overflowing with gratitude, stammered out his thanks and said, 'May God reward you, sir' – why then Tummeldink would curl up his lips into a scornful smile, and answer, 'I don't need God's reward. I have enough of everything.'

So when the time came for Tummeldink to die, his spirit found itself in a quandary. He went up to heaven, and St Peter, who as you know is God's gatekeeper, said, 'Oh, so you are the fellow who doesn't want God's reward? No, I can't let you in; for to dwell in heaven is God's reward.'

Then Mr Tummeldink went down to hell. But Satan said, '*What*, come in here! Certainly not! The voices of all those people who have asked God to reward you have dinned in my ears for long enough. Be off, and let me hear no more of such unpleasant prattle!'

What was Tummeldink to do? Where was Tummeldink to go, poor forlorn spectre that he was? He went back to earth, and sat down outside the great mansion that had once been his home, and he wept. And when on moonlit nights, or starry nights, people going home to bed saw him, they got a shock, I can tell you! Women screamed and ran; and even the bravest of brave men felt their hearts give a thump as they hurried past.

'Oh, what am I to do, what *am* I to do, and where am I to go?' wept Tummeldink.

Now you must know that every one of us, even the worst and most selfish of us, has a good angel. And though Tummeldink's good angel was very small and humble, and never in all Tummeldink's earthly life had been able to speak above a whisper, or make Tummeldink listen to those whispers, still the good little angel did not desert Tummeldink now.

'Tummeldink,' said the good little angel, coming to sit down by his side, 'I'm afraid things are not going exactly well with you.'

'Oh, get along with your nonsense,' growled Tummeldink. '*Not exactly well*, indeed! You know perfectly well that they couldn't be going worse! Heaven won't have me, Hell won't have me. And when I come back to earth people scream and run.'

Then the good little angel touched Tummeldink with his gentle hand, and turned him into a ball of fire. And the angel carried that ball of fire out of the town, and over fields and moors and past villages and solitary farms, to a place where four roads met. One road was smooth and broad, one road was steep and narrow; one was all twists and corners, one was swampy and crowded with bushes. And here the good little angel set down the ball of fire that was Tummeldink, and said, 'Shine here by night and lead tired travellers home.'

And when he had said that, the good little angel spread his wings and flew away.

Well, there you are. At first the grumpy and bad-tempered Tummeldink, even though he was now a bright and burning light, didn't want to lead anyone home. He just sat there by the roadside and sulked. Until, one dark and stormy night, a poor woman came along. The woman had a baby in her arms, and was leading a little boy by the hand, and the little boy was crying.

'I'm tired, Mumma, I'm tired,' wailed the little boy. 'My feets hurt, I want to go ho-ome!'

'Well, so we are going home,' said the woman.

But she stopped walking and looked about her uncertainly. It was plain to see that she didn't know which way to take.

And then something stirred in Tummeldink's heart that had never stirred there before. And that was pity. And he rose up shining like any full moon on a cloudless night.

'Ah, *now* I see our way!' cried the woman joyfully. 'Now we'll soon be home! Come along, little son!'

And there she was hurrying along the road that was all twists and turns, with the baby clasped in her arms, the little boy clinging to her skirt, and the bright and burning light that was Tummeldink going on before her, shedding a radiance over every inch of the road, and waiting at every corner for the woman to catch up with him.

And when he had seen her safe to her cottage, and she had gone in and shut the door and lighted a lamp, Tummeldink went back to the lonely place where the four roads met. But he wasn't sulking any more, he was smiling.

'Oh, my little good angel,' he said aloud, 'oh, my little good angel, *now* I know what I must do!'

And after that, travellers on moonless nights in lonely places, groping their way along, would suddenly see in front of them a fiery light, burning like a bundle of straw, and leaping up and down. At first people were scared when they saw the light, but by and by they came to welcome it. For if, lost in darkness, they didn't know which way to turn, they had only to say, 'Come, light me home!' And there was the little light dancing ahead of them, and shedding radiance all along the way. They got to look upon that little light as a matter of course. But though they watched for it and welcomed it, there was never a traveller among them who thought to thank it.

Until – now listen carefully – for now we are coming to the climax of the story.

There was a farmer, and he had ridden to market, and done a

good stroke of business over the sale of his horse. And after that, being well pleased with himself, he had spent a merry evening with his fellows in a tavern. Now, late at night, he was going home on foot, and it came on to rain. Indeed it was a regular storm of rain: the sky was black with clouds, there wasn't a peep of a star or a glim of a moon to light him on his way.

Well, the farmer knew his way well enough. And he was ambling along a flat road, jingling his money in his pocket and trolling out a tuneless song, when his foot tripped on a stone, and he lost his balance, and tumbled head over heels into a deep ditch that lay along the left hand side of the road. The ditch, owing to the rain, was a regular swamp and full of water. And there was our farmer, struggling for a foothold and finding none, and sinking ever deeper and deeper into the muddy water. 'If only little Tummeldink were here to light me out of this accursed swamp!' he thought.

And then, fearing he was about to drown, he gave a yell. 'Tummeldink, little Tummeldink!' he yelled. 'For mercy's sake show me a light!'

No sooner had he spoken those words than a light shone over the swamp, and there was the little blazing ball of fire shining steadily above the farmer's head, and showing him where to take a hold with his hands, and where to set his feet against the side of the ditch; and there was the farmer scrambling out of the ditch and standing on the road again.

And then what did the little light do? It went dancing along the road, and the farmer followed it, and so came safely home.

At the door of his house the farmer paused with his hand on the latch. 'I've a-plenty of money in my pockets, Mester Tummeldink,' he said. 'And you should have it all – only I reckon that money ain't no use to the likes of you. So all I can do, Mester Tummeldink, is to thank 'ee kindly. And may God reward you for this night's work.'

And then the farmer's eyes goggled and his mouth gaped. For the little burning light that was Tummeldink was rising into the air. Up, up, up it went: the wind battered against it, the rain pelted it, but neither wind nor rain could dim that little light. Up and up and up

it went, to the very gate of heaven. And then it turned into Tummeldink. And Tummeldink knocked meekly at Heaven's gate.

It was St Peter who opened the gate. 'Well, Tummeldink – you here again! And what have you come for this time?'

'I – I don't quite know,' stammered Tummeldink. 'There was a fellow down on earth who – who spoke some words.'

St Peter smiled. 'I know the words he spoke. Come in now, Tummeldink!'

So Tummeldink went in through Heaven's gate.

13 · Tangletop

1. The Haystacks

A farmer had three sons. The eldest was called Ernst, the second was called Heinz, and the youngest – well, I can't tell you what his real name was: everyone called him Tangletop, because he had such a mop of goldy-yellow hair.

Tangletop was good-natured and easy going. His two elder brothers despised him and thought him a 'dummling' or 'stupid head.' However, he wasn't such a dummling as they supposed – as this story will prove.

The farmer – the father of these three lads – had many hayfields. But those hayfields weren't of any use to him, because every year, after the hay was stacked, someone came in the night and stole it all. Nobody knew who the thief was, no one had ever seen him: one evening the hay would be all neatly stacked in a field at the back of the house, and next morning it was gone.

Now in the year that this story is going to tell you about, there had been a particularly good hay harvest; the farmer and his three sons were kept busy cutting and carting it. And on a day towards the end of the summer, there were three great haystacks standing in a field behind the farmhouse. The farmer looked at these three stacks gloomily.

'If we lose the hay again we shall be in queer street and will have to borrow money to carry on,' he said. 'I'd give a new pair of shoes and a new linen coat to anyone who could catch the thief.'

The farmer's eldest son, Ernst, thought he would very much like a new pair of shoes and a new linen coat. So he said he would watch in the field all night. 'I'll take my gun,' said he. 'And if the thief *does* come – well, let him look out, that's all!'

So that night Ernst took his gun and went to sit down under the hedge in the field. He thought it would be easy to stay awake, but it wasn't. The night breeze blew softly, the grasses rustled about his feet. Soon his head began to nod, and his eyes kept shutting. He hadn't been sitting there one hour when he was fast, fast asleep.

Oh, alas! When he fell asleep there had been three haystacks standing in the field. But when he woke next morning there were only two.

Sadly he went back into the farmhouse and told his father. The farmer shrugged his shoulders. 'I didn't expect anything else,' he said.

But Heinz, the second brother, exclaimed, 'A pretty sort of watchman you! Tonight *I'll* keep watch! *My* head shan't nod, and *my* eyes shan't close! If the thief comes again, he'll get a bullet through his heart!'

And that night Heinz took a gun, and went to sit under the hedge in the field.

The night breeze blew softly, the grasses rustled about his feet. Soon his head began to nod, and his eyes kept shutting. In less than an hour he was fast, fast asleep.

Oh, alas! When he fell asleep there had been two big haystacks standing in the field. When he woke up next morning there was only one.

Sadly he went back into the farm kitchen and told his father.

The farmer shrugged his shoulders. 'Same this year as last year,' he said. 'Seems it's my fate.'

Then Tangletop, who was sitting at the table, golloping up his porridge with great enjoyment, put down his spoon and said, 'What is fate? Only something that happens. And why shouldn't it happen differently? I think tonight it will be my turn to watch.'

'*You!*' said Ernst.

'*You!*' said Heinz.

And they both laughed.

'Well, if I can't do better, I can't do worse,' said Tangletop.

And he, too, laughed.

That evening Tangletop took a comb and a length of thin rope with him into the field. He made one end of the rope fast to the haystack, and the other end of the rope fast to the comb. Then he stuck the comb in his hair, and went to sit down under the hedge.

The night breeze blew softly, the grasses rustled about his feet. Tangletop shut his eyes, he didn't even try to keep awake. Soon he was fast, fast asleep.

By and by a full moon rose behind the farmhouse. Now it was shining down into the field, lighting up the short turf, casting a long shadow of the one remaining haystack across the grass, and gleaming on Tangletop's great mop of goldy-yellow hair, as he lay curled up sound asleep under the hedge.

And then suddenly – *scratch*, *scratch* went the comb in Tangletop's mop of yellow hair. *Scratch*, *scratch!* The comb jumped out of Tangletop's hair, and Tangletop sat up, wide awake, and staring with all his eyes. What was he seeing? He was seeing a very small grey Spook standing by the haystack, pulling the hay out of the stack, and loading it on to a very big brown horse.

'Oh no, you don't!' shouted Tangletop.

And he jumped to his feet and ran to the haystack.

The little grey Spook gave one glance over his shoulder, sprang, light as a bird, on to the back of the big brown horse, and galloped out of the field, with Tangletop racing after him.

The horse galloped, Tangletop ran, out of the field, away and away in the silent moonlit night, away on the road that led to the forest. Not a sound did the horse's hoofs make on the road: the only sound was the *thud*, *thud*, *thud* of Tangletop's running feet in their clumsy boots. He was getting left behind, but he could still see the shadowy horse going on in front of him, and he ran, ran, *ran* with all his might towards the forest and into the forest, where the moonlight glanced down between the trees on to the galloping horse, and on to the small grey head of the little shadowy Spook who sat on the horse's back.

And all at once the trees fell back on either side, and Tangletop found himself standing in a wide clearing, where the moon was shining down on to the white walls of a magnificent palace. The little grey Spook was scrambling off the horse's back. Tangletop was breathless with running, but he made a leap, caught the little Spook by the shoulders and shook him vigorously.

'You little rat!' he panted. 'You rotten little thief! I could kill you! How dare you come stealing my father's hay?'

'Oh, oh, oh!' whimpered the little grey Spook. 'You're hurting me! Let me go and I'll give you my brown horse!'

'All right,' said Tangletop, 'I'll come and fetch it in the early morning. And I'll bring a cart to carry back all the hay you've stolen. But now I must return to my watch in the field. And I warn you, if you dare to come stealing my father's hay again, it will be the worse for you!'

'Oh no, no, I won't come again,' said the little Spook. 'I don't want your hay – it was only my fun.'

'Fun!' said Tangletop. 'A pretty fine sort of fun!'

And he turned and went back to the field. And there, having picked up the comb, and put it back into his hair, and having made sure that one end of the rope was fast to the comb, and the other end fast to the haystack, he sat down under the hedge, yawned, blinked once or twice, shut his eyes, opened his eyes, shut them again, and – oh dear me – again he fell asleep.

He's dreaming that he's galloping about the world on the back of the Spook's big brown horse, when suddenly – *scratch, scratch, scratch* goes the comb again in Tangletop's goldy-yellow hair. Tangletop wakes, rubs his eyes, scrambles to his feet. Well, did you ever? There's that rascally little Spook back in the field again, hurriedly pulling the hay out of the stack, and loading it on to the back of a big *white* horse.

Tangletop gives a yell, the little Spook jumps on to the horse's back, and away with him galloping off towards the forest, with Tangletop chasing after him.

Again they come to the clearing in the forest, and again Tangletop gets a grip of the little Spook, just as he's scrambling off the horse's back.

'Now I really will kill you!' shouts Tangletop.

Tangletop ought to have remembered that you can't kill a Spook, because a Spook is neither flesh nor blood but only shadow. But

he was too angry to think of that; and the Spook was too frightened to remind him of it. All the Spook did was to promise not to come stealing any more hay, to return all he had stolen, to give Tangletop his white horse, and to bring both the brown and the white horses to the field in the morning.

So Tangletop goes back to the field. But he doesn't fall asleep this time. He doesn't even sit down under the hedge. He walks up and down, up and down, keeping an eye on the haystack. And he hasn't been walking up and down very long, when he sees that rascally little Spook back again, pulling the hay out of the stack, and loading it on to the back of a big black horse.

Tangletop gives a yell, he rushes to the haystack, the little Spook scrambles on to the back of the big black horse, he's away galloping towards the forest, and into the forest, with Tangletop racing after him. They come to the clearing, and this time Tangletop makes a grab at the little Spook just as he is scrambling off the horse. Now he has that little Spook by the neck – or thinks he has; but what he is grasping is only empty air, and the little Spook slides out of Tangletop's hands, and slithers to the ground.

'Ho! ho!' cries the little Spook. 'I like you, Tangletop! I do like you! You and I ought to be friends.'

'Friends!' cries Tangletop. '*Friends* – you little sneak who comes stealing all our hay!'

'Well, I won't do it again,' says the little Spook. 'It was more a joke than anything. Tell you what, Tangletop, you can have my palace if you fancy it. You come and have a look round my palace. It's really handsome, but I'm lonely. And if you'll come and live in my palace, now and then, just for a bit of company, I promise you I'll serve you faithfully.'

'Well, I suppose I may as well have a look now I'm here,' said Tangletop, scarcely knowing whether he was awake or dreaming.

And he went with the little Spook into the palace.

Certainly that palace was no dream! It was as real as could be, and fitted out magnificently, quite beyond anything that Tangletop could ever have imagined. And when he had seen all over it and come out again the little Spook made him a low bow and handed him the key of the entrance door. Then he said, 'Yours to command. My name's Rumpen Trumpen; when you want me, call me.'

'But what about Father's hay?' said Tangletop.

'Don't you fret yourself about that,' said the little Spook. 'I'll put it back. But the sun will soon be rising. You best go home. Quick now . . . '

Whizz, bang!

What happened after that, Tangletop could never remember. One moment he was standing outside the Spook's palace, the next moment he was squeezed up against the hedge in the hay field, with the little golden key of the Spook's palace in his hand. There was scarcely room for him to move because in the field stood more than a hundred haystacks. Yes, all the hay that had been stolen through the years was back again.

'*Won't* Father be pleased!' exclaimed Tangletop. 'But what's this I've got hold of? Oh, of course, the key to the palace . . . Better not let anyone see that. If Father and Ernst and Heinz get a hold of the key, they'll want to take over the palace and boss me.'

So he tied the key to a strand of his golden hair, pulled a whole lot of hair over it, and went into the farm kitchen, where he found his father and his brothers at breakfast.

'Father,' says he, 'I've got all the hay back. And I don't think it will ever be stolen again.'

And that's all he did say. However much his father and his brothers questioned him, not a word more could they get out of him.

2. *The Cave at the World's End*

'Father,' said Tangletop that evening. 'I've been thinking. I'm not much use about the farm, am I?'

'No use at all,' said his father, 'when it comes to work.'

'Worse than useless, if you ask me,' said Ernst.

'Mooning about and getting in everyone's way,' said Heinz.

'That's just it,' said Tangletop. 'So I've a mind to leave you for a bit – to seek my fortune, as they say.'

'My poor dear lad, are you crazy?' said his father.

'Let him go, let him go!' said Ernst.

'And a good riddance!' said Heinz.

'Nay, nay, my lads, that's not fair,' said the farmer. 'Remember who got our hay back for us. Though I do think, Tangletop, you needn't be so secretive as to how you did it.'

Tangletop made no answer to that. It was his secret, and he meant to keep it. He just said goodbye to his father and his brothers, and walked away. Where did he go? To his palace in the forest to be sure. And there he lived happily for a while, with the Spook cooking him such delicious meals as he'd never had in all his life, and seeing to the making of his bed, and the washing of his clothes, and the darning of his stockings.

But by and by Tangletop got bored.

'I don't know how it is,' he said to the Spook one day. 'I seem to have everything – and yet there is something lacking. I feel like a silly frog that's forever croaking, "I want, I want, I don't know what I want!" '

'I know what you want,' said the Spook. 'It's a wife.'

'So it is!' said Tangletop. 'How come I didn't think of that before?'

'If you ask me, thinking isn't your strong point,' said the Spook. 'Now listen. I know the very wife for you, but – '

'But *what*?' said Tangletop, all impatience.

'Oh well,' said the Spook, 'I was just wondering if you were brave enough.'

'If you dare call me a coward, I'll wring that skinny neck of yours!' shouted Tangletop.

'Now, now,' laughed the Spook, 'don't get excited. You know I haven't got the sort of neck you *can* wring. And I didn't call you a coward. But there are different kinds of bravery. There's the bravery you need to stand up for yourself; and there's the bravery that would make you feel sick with fear to do a thing, and yet to do it.'

'Stop gabbling,' said Tangletop, 'and tell me what's in your mind.'

'At the World's End,' said the Spook, 'there's a cave. And in that cave there is a beautiful enchanted princess, who would make you such a wife as your heart could desire. And all that is needed to free her from enchantment is to give her three kisses.'

'And you think that to kiss a princess would make me feel sick!' exclaimed Tangletop.

'Wait till you see her,' said the Spook gloomily.

'But you told me she was beautiful,' said Tangletop.

'So she is – sometimes,' said the Spook. 'Well, I suppose you better be off. I'll tell the white horse the way – no good telling you, you'd only lose yourself . . . Oh, so you want to go this minute, do you?' he said, as Tangletop jumped up and hurried out to the stable.

'I'll need a pillion to bring the princess back on,' said Tangletop.

'*If* you bring her back,' said the Spook.

'Of course I shall bring her back!' cried Tangletop.

And there he was, saddling and bridling the white horse, and arranging a soft cushiony pillion for the princess behind the saddle.

Meanwhile the Spook and the white horse were talking together, in a language that was all neighs and wuff, wuff, wuffles. And the white horse was nodding his head, as if he thoroughly understood.

And then the Spook gave Tangletop a little hamper containing a bottle of wine and some sandwiches. 'Eat when you're hungry, and drink when you're thirsty,' said the Spook. 'The hamper will fill itself up again. Now off you go. *Hope* to see you again some day!'

Then Tangletop jumped on to the back of the white horse and galloped away. The Spook stood at the palace gate looking after him and smiling. It was the first time since the world began that the Spook had ever felt fond of anyone. And why he felt fond of Tangletop he really didn't know. But it gave him a warm happy sort of feeling in the place where his heart, if he had possessed such a thing, should be.

The white horse, with Tangletop astride him, was galloping, galloping. That horse never seemed to tire, though Tangletop himself often wearied, and sometimes wished himself back in his palace with the Spook. But in a long time – or a short time, according to how you reckon time – they came to the World's End. And the white horse pulled up before the entrance to a cave.

'Do I get down here?' said Tangletop.

The white horse nodded his head.

'And do I go into the cave?' said Tangletop.

The white horse nodded his head.

'And you'll wait for me?' said Tangletop.

The white horse nodded his head.

So Tangletop dismounted and went into the cave.

At first it was so dark inside that cave that he could see nothing. Then there came a little light, like a candle flame, at the farther end of the cave. Now Tangletop was groping his way towards that light, and all the time it was getting brighter and brighter, until he reached the end of the cave, and found himself standing in a regular dazzle of light before a golden throne.

And on the throne sat a lion, and the lion roared out, 'Give me a kiss!'

'Well, old fellow,' said Tangletop, 'you're not exactly what I came to the World's End to see. But if you want a kiss – here goes!'

And he kissed the lion on his tawny muzzle.

Then slowly, slowly a green curtain fell between himself and the lion. And slowly, slowly the green curtain rose again. And now on the golden throne sat a white-horned goat.

'Give me a kiss,' bleated the white-horned goat.

'Anything to oblige,' said Tangletop.

And he kissed the goat on its hairy forehead.

Slowly, slowly the green curtain fell. Slowly, slowly it rose again. And there on the golden throne sat an enormous snake.

'Give me a kiss-ss-ss!' hissed the snake.

Oh, how could he, how could he? Tangletop took a step back. He was terrified. He felt like running out of the cave. Then he remembered the Spook's words: 'There's a bravery that would make you feel sick with fear to do a thing, and yet to do it.' And in desperation he dashed up to the golden throne and kissed the snake on its open mouth.

A flash of lightning, a peal of thunder, the cave lit up from end to end. And there on the golden throne sat – no terrible snake but a princess more beautiful than Tangletop had ever imagined that anyone could possibly be.

The princess was smiling, the princess was laughing, she was stepping down from the golden throne and holding out both her pretty white hands.

'Oh, my deliverer, oh, my dearest love!' cried the princess. 'How long have I awaited you! And how dreary, dreary has been the waiting!'

Now she was in Tangletop's arms; and Tangletop, beside himself with joy, was kissing her again and again, and forgetting where he was, and who he was, and everything else in the world, except that he held the princess in his arms.

But outside the cave the white horse was neighing and stamping. And the princess laughed and said, 'Dear Tangletop, isn't it time you took me home?'

'Yes,' said Tangletop, 'I will take you home.'

Hand in hand they went out of the cave; and Tangletop lifted the princess on to the back of the white horse, and got up in front of her. Now the white horse was galloping, galloping; and after a long time, which seemed a short time to Tangletop in his happiness, they arrived at the palace in the forest, and found the little Spook at the palace gate, waiting to welcome them.

So our story reaches its end, with the wedding of Tangletop and the princess. Of course Tangletop's father and his two brothers were invited to the wedding, and they came: the two brothers all humble apologies, and Tangletop's father quite bewildered in his pride of his youngest son, and his regret at having misjudged him.

'But I did stick up for him when his brothers tried to run him down,' thought the old man – and found some consolation in the thought.

14 · *The Spook and the Pigs*

Once upon a time a Spook was wandering about the world. You wouldn't have known him for a Spook because he had disguised himself as a poor traveller. And in this disguise he came to a roadside inn.

The innkeeper was standing at his door, on the look-out for customers.

'Good day, sir,' says the Spook.

'Good day,' says the innkeeper.

'The sun is very hot,' says the Spook.

'So it seems,' says the innkeeper.

'And I am very thirsty,' says the Spook. 'Could you spare a poor traveller a drink of beer?'

'Certainly,' says the innkeeper. 'If you've the money to pay for it.'

'Alas, alas, sir,' says the Spook, 'my pockets are empty.'

'And wouldn't *my* pockets soon be empty, if I ladled out free drinks to every beggar on the road?' says the innkeeper. 'You take yourself off, before you feel my stick across your back!'

'My back is aching sore enough without having any blows added to it,' said the Spook.

And he hobbled away, saying to himself, 'A hard heart needs a sharp lesson.'

Now the innkeeper had a hay field. And the hay had been cut and was gathered into tidy stooks, ready for carting. And when the Spook saw those stooks he said a few magic words, and changed all the stooks into pigs. Then he took on the likeness of a farmer, and drove the pigs back to the inn.

The innkeeper was still standing at his door. And when he saw the pigs he said, 'Selling them, are you?'

'If I can get a good price for them,' said the Spook-farmer.

The innkeeper offered a sum of money.

The Spook-farmer shook his head.

The innkeeper offered a bigger sum of money.

The Spook-farmer shook his head.

The innkeeper offered a still bigger sum. 'And that's my last word,' he said.

'Oh, all right,' said the Spook-farmer. 'But, mind you, you're getting the best of the bargain.'

The innkeeper made no answer. But he thought to himself, 'If I didn't always get the best of the bargain – where should I be?'

And he bought the pigs – little knowing that he was paying out money for his own hay!

The Spook pocketed the money, and said, 'There's just one thing I ought to tell you about those pigs. Let them drink from a trough, and not from running water.'

'I don't need any instructions from *you* on the way to manage them,' said the innkeeper. 'They'll drink just where I choose to let them drink.'

'Well, you can't say I haven't warned you,' said the Spook-farmer.

And he went briskly on his way, chuckling to himself.

The pigs were squealing and snuffling about the innkeeper's yard. They were evidently thirsty. 'Pah!' said the innkeeper. 'As if I were going to waste my time filling troughs for the likes of you!' And he called his lad to look out for customers, whilst he himself drove the pigs down to a stream that flowed through a meadow behind the inn.

The pigs ran to the stream – and then what happened? Each pig as its snout touched the water turned into a bundle of hay; and the stream caught those bundles of hay and whirled them away and away.

Shouting and yelling and shaking his fists the innkeeper waded into the stream; but the bundles of hay were gone far beyond his reach.

And when the innkeeper next went to look at his hay field, he found that all the hay stooks had gone also: which of course just shows you how dangerous it is to treat anyone – even the seemingly poorest of poor travellers – with disrespect.

15 · The Spectre Wolf

The Spectre Wolf was huge and fierce; but he moved lightly as all spectres do. All you could hear when he was prowling round in the wood was *pit-pat*, *pit-a-pat*, a sound like rain dripping on to fallen leaves.

Outside the wood was a meadow, and beyond the meadow was a small house. And one summer morning as the Spectre Wolf was coming out of the wood, *pit-pat*, *pit-a-pat*, he saw a pretty little girl in the garden of the house, picking flowers. 'Ah,' thought the Spectre Wolf, 'that little girl would make me a nice little dinner!' and he licked his shadowy lips.

There was a high fence round the garden; and before the little girl's father had gone off to work, he said, 'Letty, my honey, mind you don't go outside the garden till I come home, lest that old Spectre Wolf should snap you up.'

'No, Dadda, I won't go out of the garden,' said Letty.

And Letty didn't mean to go outside the garden. But there, what would you? There were such pretty flowers *just* outside the garden gate: prettier, Letty thought, than any flowers *inside* the gate. 'So I'll just step outside for a minute or two,' says she to herself. 'I can always run back quick if I see Mr Spectre Wolf coming along.'

And she laid down the flowers she had been picking, and went out through the gate to pick those prettier ones. Goldy-white they were, and flickering in the sun and wind.

Well, she was just about stooping to pick those goldy-white flowers, when she saw some even prettier ones a little farther off. Some of them were rosy pink, and some of them were blue. They were like the two colours in the sky when the sun's rising on a clear morning. She was about to pick those prettier flowers when –

well, there, did you ever? – she saw some even prettier farther off, and beyond those again some prettier still; and so she was going on and on, and getting farther and farther from the safety of her own garden.

Now she was singing a sweet happy little song, in her sweet happy little voice. And then she heard a sound that wasn't the sound of her own voice, nor the rustling of the grasses round her feet, nor the morning song of the birds: *pit-pat*, *pit-a-pat*: the light prowling tread of the Spectre Wolf.

She turned to run home then. But the Spectre Wolf called out, 'Letty, don't you move!'

'Oh no, dear Mr Wolf, I-I wouldn't think of moving,' says Letty all of a tremble.

'Letty,' says the Spectre Wolf, 'sing that sweet pretty little song again.'

So Letty began to sing again. But she was so frightened that she couldn't get the words right, and what she sang sounded like '*Tray-bla, tray-bla, cum-qua, kimo!*'

And as she sang, she was taking little steps, such little, little steps, backwards towards her home.

'Letty,' says the Spectre Wolf, 'you're moving.'

'Oh no, dear Mr Wolf,' says Letty, 'why should I move?'

'Well then, Letty,' says the Spectre Wolf, 'if you're not moving, sing that sweet pretty little song again.'

Letty's lips were trembling, and her voice would come no louder than the peep-peep of a little unfledged bird. And it was the same nonsensical words she was singing: '*Tray-bla, tray-bla, cum-qua-kimo.*' And all the time she was singing, she was taking one step, and then another step, backwards towards her home.

'LETTY,' howls the Spectre Wolf, 'YOU'RE MOVING!'

'Oh no, dear Mr Wolf! Why should I move?'

'Well then, Letty, sing some more.'

So then Letty began to sing again: '*Tray-bla, tray-bla, cum-qua-kimo.*' And the Wolf sat down, and cocked his head on one side, and shut his eyes the better to listen. And when Letty saw that his eyes were shut, she took heart, the strength came back to her legs, and she turned and made a dash for home, with the flowers dropping from her hands as she ran.

'Letty,' said the Spectre Wolf, 'how come you're not singing?'

Then he heard the slam of the garden gate, and he opened his eyes.

'*Ow-ow-ow, erow-erow-erow!*' Now he was racing after Letty, and howling. He got to the garden gate and floated over it. He went whizzing up the garden path to the house door. He sprang at the door, but Letty had locked it. What matter? Now his spectral head was coming in under the door, and his spectral body would have followed it, had not Letty bethought herself to snatch up her Dadda's Bible and hold it out in front of her.

No, the Spectre Wolf couldn't face that Bible. So he went back to the wood with his tail between his legs, and mournfully howling: '*Ow-o-o-ow! E-row-e-row-row-row!*'

16 · *The Inn of the Stone and Spectre*

On a wet and windy evening a scissors grinder was toiling along a country road, pushing his little grinding machine before him. He was tired and hungry, and had still many a mile to go before he reached the town where he had a friend who he knew would give him shelter for the night.

'What I need,' thought the poor fellow, 'is a drop of something strong to put heart into me.'

And he had scarcely thought that thought when, at a turn of the road, he came across a big inn with lights blazing from many a window, and a signboard swaying in the wind.

The signboard had a lamp over it, so that the name of the inn, printed in large bold lettering, was plain to read. And the name was this:

THE STONE AND SPECTRE

The scissors grinder left his grinding machine at the door, and stepped inside. Soon he was seated before a blazing fire in the bar room, with a glass of brandy on a table beside him, but with nothing at all in his pockets, for he had paid for that glass of brandy with his last coppers. He was falling into a half doze when the landlord, a great, strapping, handsome fellow, came up to him and said, 'Sir, you look but poorly, and we have a comfortable bed vacant. What about putting up here for the night?'

The scissors grinder gave a weary smile. 'Can't afford it,' he said. 'Pockets empty.'

'Oh, that doesn't signify,' answered the landlord. 'Beds are free here to those who need them.'

'Free!' exclaimed the scissors grinder. '*Free!* You – you can't mean it!'

'But I do mean it,' answered the landlord. 'Supper's free too.'

Then he went away, and soon came back again, carrying a tray piled up with a bowl of soup, a dish of meat and mashed potatoes, and a goodly helping of plum pudding.

The scissors grinder thought he must be dreaming. But he was so hungry that he gobbled up everything, quicker than quick, whilst the landlord drew up a chair to the fire and sat watching him, and smiling.

'Shall I tell you a bit of a story?' said the landlord.

The scissors grinder nodded.

'But first I'll introduce you to my brothers,' said the landlord. And he gave a low whistle.

Then in came three more tall handsome fellows, so like the landlord that you couldn't doubt they were his brothers. These three also drew up their chairs to the fire, and the landlord began his story:

'Some years ago – no matter how many or how few – we four brothers were Hussars in the service of a king. And one summer morning we were standing on guard outside the king's palace. Close by the palace – in fact just across the road that led up to the palace gates – was a lake. And as the day was very hot, and we were very young and foolish, what must we do but strip and into the lake, all four of us, for a swim.

'Well, there we were, splashing about in the water, merry as you please, when we heard the sound of trotting hoofs and the little clatter of carriage wheels in the distance, but coming every moment nearer. And then – heaven help us! – we saw that it was the King's coach, with the King himself sitting inside it.

'We were out of the water in a flash, snatching up our swords, ramming the shakos on to our heads, and back to our posts. But before we had time to put on our uniforms, or even so much as our shirts, the carriage came driving swiftly up to us. So we stood up straight, all naked as we were, and presented arms as the carriage swept past.

'Naturally the King was furious. And no sooner had he stepped into his palace than he sent an officer to arrest us. But we meanwhile had hurried into our uniforms, and when we saw the officer coming we took to our heels and fled into the forest. And there, for the whole summer through, we stayed hidden in a forester's empty hut, with nothing to eat but berries and roots, and nothing to drink but water from a little stream that flowed past the hut.

'For a long time we dared not venture out of the forest, because the King in his rage had surrounded it with soldiers in order to catch us.

'But, at the end of that year, the King had more pressing matters for his soldiers to attend to, being threatened by an insurrection of some of his rascally subjects. So he withdrew the guard from the forest. When we overheard some charcoal burners talking about all this, we debated between ourselves whether we should return to the palace and offer our service in helping to quell the insurrection, but concluded that it was more than likely that by so doing we should find ourselves being strung up on the gallows, for the King was not one to forgive offences.

'However, here was our chance to get clean away. So, one moonless night, we ventured out of the forest, on the opposite side to the King's palace.

'All night we were hurrying along a highroad, not knowing or caring much where it might lead us. And just before dawn we heard a curious moaning sound, as of someone in great distress or pain. The sound brought us to a halt; and looking about us, we saw in a field at the side of the road, a great shadowy Spectre. The Spectre was bending over a big stone, trying, as it seemed, to move it. And it was crying out in a voice fit to break your heart, "I can't. I must! I can't, I can't, I *must*!"

'Well, you might suppose that such a sight would send us scurrying on our way; but somehow it didn't. It moved us to pity. And I, being the eldest of us four brothers, stepped over to the Spectre, and asked what ailed it, adding that if we could help it in any way, it had only to say the word.

'The Spectre looked up. Tears began to trickle down its shadowy face. And, believe me, those tears seemed more real and substantial than all the rest of its shadowy self. "Oh, such a sad story," it wept. "Oh, such a sad, sad story!"

' "Tell me your story," said I.

'And with sobs and sighs and ineffectual jerkings at the big stone with its frail shadowy hands, the Spectre told:

' "When I was a man, as other men, I was rich. I bought land and built me a fine house. Oh, I had land enough, but I was greedy and craved for more. And in the night I moved one of the boundary stones between my neighbour's land and mine. Every night I moved it a yard or two – only a yard or two at a time, so that no one need notice. I reckoned that by this means I should in years have added a goodly acreage to the property I owned. But I had moved it less than a quarter of a mile when death came for me. And now the justice of heaven will grant me no rest until I have put the stone back in its proper place. Day and night I strive to move it, but it is heavy and I am frail. Day and night for fifty years I have laboured at my task. But I have not yet moved the stone one inch – no, not one inch!"

' "Well," said I, "if that's all your trouble, it's soon remedied. Here we are, four of us brothers, all strong and lusty fellows. Show me where the stone should be, and we will move it for you."

'Then I called my brothers, and with the Spectre leading the way, we all four set to work to push the stone uphill into an adjoining field. When we got it there, the Spectre was still shedding tears; but now they were tears of joy.

' "I can go to my rest, I can go to my rest!" he cried in his quavering voice, that sounded like the wind stirring through a field of corn.

'Then he began slowly, slowly to rise into the air, as you might see a cloud rising when the wind blows over a hill. But he hadn't risen far, when he floated down again, to hover just above our heads.

' "There is a treasure which is mine," he said, "truly and honestly mine. I buried it close to where the stone now is, under the hedge.

Dig! You will not have far to dig. In return for what you have done for me, I bestow this treasure upon you. And all I ask is that you make good honest use of it."

'And so having said, the Spectre rose up into the air again, and vanished into the blue of heaven.

'Well, between us, we four brothers had soon unearthed that treasure. What was it? It was four big sacks brim full of gold coins. So, each carrying a sack, we went on our way. And when we had crossed the border between our king's kingdom and the next, and so had no further fear of arrest, we spent the gold in building this inn.

'So now you see,' added the landlord with a chuckle, 'why it is called THE STONE AND SPECTRE, and why, in gratitude, we are always ready to give free bed and board to those who have no money to pay for it.'

17 · *The Little Old Man in the Tree*

Once upon a time there were two brothers, Daniel and Mark, who lived in a little cottage by the sea, and earned their living by fishing. To be sure it wasn't much they earned, but it was just enough to keep them in food and clothes: until – oh dear! – they fell in love with two pretty girls, and wanted to get married. That made all the difference; because those two pretty girls were just as poor as Daniel and Mark. And how could four people live on earnings that were only just enough to keep two?

'We must hope for the best, brother,' said Mark.

'And in the meantime put up with the worst,' said Daniel gloomily.

Well now, one fine morning they put out to sea as usual, and when they came to the fishing ground they cast their net overboard. But when they pulled in the net, it was empty. They cast the net out again and again, and still they caught nothing. They fished all day: now it was late afternoon, now it was sunset, now it was twilight; and still they had caught nothing.

'Seems we're to go supperless to bed this night, brother,' said Daniel.

'Oh come,' said Mark, 'not quite supperless! We've half a loaf of bread and a crust of cheese in the larder. And now – just one more throw, for luck!'

And they cast in their net.

'Empty again!' said Daniel, as they pulled the net in. 'Oh, hullo, hullo – not quite empty! Well, did you ever see anything like this!'

And he put his hand into the net, and took out the most beautiful little fish that shone in the twilight with all the colours of the rainbow.

'A pity to eat that!' said Mark, taking the little fish from Daniel. 'Oh – er – I – I beg your pardon, sir,' he exclaimed in astonishment. For believe it or not, that little fish began to speak.

'Yes, Mark, it would be a great pity to eat me. Because I should certainly make you very ill. But, on the other hand, if you will spare my life, I promise you I will make your fortunes. Now, now don't stare at me like that. Put me back in the water, *at once*!'

Splash! Mark dropped the little fish overboard. 'It – it spoke brother,' he said, feeling quite bewildered.

'Yes, it spoke,' said Daniel, equally bewildered. 'Oh, see – here it is, putting its head up out of the water! And – oh hark, it's speaking again!'

The little fish had its head up out of the water, and its voice came clear and shrill above the lapping of the waves against the boat. 'You fellows, are you listening?'

'Yes, we – we are listening,' stammered Mark.

'Then come here to the beach early tomorrow morning,' said the little fish. 'There will be a surprise waiting for you. Maybe that surprise will bring you a fortune; maybe not.'

Then the little fish swam away. The brothers rowed their boat ashore, beached it, made it fast, and went home through the deepening dusk to their supper of bread and cheese.

Neither of them slept very well that night. They kept dreaming of the little fish, and waking, and wondering. The dawn found them setting off for the beach. And when they got there – what did they see?

Two handsome horses, saddled and bridled and two big beautiful dogs. The horses whinnied to them; the dogs ran to them, wagging their tails. The brothers didn't think twice: they jumped on to the horses, called to the dogs, and set out into the world to seek their fortunes – one dog following close at the heels of Daniel's horse, the other close at the heels of Mark's horse.

They rode, rode, rode, and by and by they came to a place where there grew a great oak. And here the road divided: one road going to the right of the oak, the other to the left. The road to the left was broader and smoother, so they took that way. But they hadn't gone far when Daniel's horse stopped dead. And when Daniel urged him to go on, he reared, he plunged, first he was on his hind legs with his forefeet in the air, and then he was on his forefeet with his hind legs in the air. It was all Daniel could do to keep his seat; and no coaxing or scolding or urging with the whip would persuade that horse to go a step farther. It was as if an invisible barrier barred his way. And the dog that followed Daniel's horse was behaving just as strangely: he had his tail between his legs, and he kept turning his head, looking back on the road they had come, and howling.

There was nothing for it but to turn round, ride back to the oak tree, and take the other road – the one to the right.

But now it was Mark's horse that refused to budge, and Mark's dog that lay down under the oak tree and howled.

'Brother,' said Mark, 'I think there is some magic here. I think these animals know something that we do not, for you must remember how we came by them. Truly I think they are telling us that the time has come for us to part. Let us take the ways that the animals would have us: I to the left, you to the right. And let us agree to meet again, here under this oak, in a year's time. But, before parting, let us thrust our knives into the bark of the oak. If they remain there, it will be a sign that all is well. But should one of us, returning first, find that the other one's knife has fallen to the ground, it will mean that the other one is in trouble. And so he whose knife is still in the tree must ride swiftly to the rescue. Do you agree, brother Daniel?'

'Yes, brother Mark, I agree,' said Daniel.

So, having each one thrust his knife into the bark of the oak, they bade each other goodbye and took their separate ways: Mark riding to the left, Daniel taking the road to the right. And one dog followed Mark, and the other followed Daniel.

Mark, followed by one of the dogs, and riding to the left, came by and by to the castle of a noble lord. There he was kindly received, and given the job of coachman, with good wages and good food, so that the year passed pleasantly for him. Now we will leave him, well content, and see how in the meantime it is faring with Daniel, who took, if you remember, the road to the right.

On this road the horse went willingly enough, with the other dog following close at his heels, up hill, and down dale, the horse now galloping, now trotting, now, where the road rose steeply, slowing into a walk. But it seemed a desolate road, with only a few poor cottages scattered here and there, and nowhere any town or village where Daniel might hope to find harbourage for the night, or work for the morrow.

Just after sunset he was riding along a moor on the edge of a forest. It was not by any means an inviting place, this moor. It was bleak and lonely, and scattered over here and there with little piles of ashes, as if many weary travellers, before Daniel, had stopped there to light a fire and rest and refresh themselves. But Daniel was also weary, and hungry and cold. Moreover his horse had just cast a shoe, so he dismounted, left the horse to pick up what grass he might among the ash piles, and promising him better luck on the morrow, he himself set about collecting twigs and broken branches, lit a fire with his tinder box, and sat down with his back against a beech tree to eat the food which he carried in his knapsack.

Well, he hadn't taken many mouthfuls when he heard a cracked old voice whimpering above his head.

'O-oh, how cold I am, how c-cold!' whimpered the cracked old voice.

And looking up, he saw a little old man in a white shirt huddled among the branches of the beech tree.

'C-cold, c-cold, I am c-cold!' whimpered the little old man again.

'Well then, little grandfather, come down and warm yourself by my fire,' said Daniel.

'No, no, no!' whimpered the old man. 'I daren't come down! Your horse will kick me, and your dog will bite me!'

'Not they, little grandfather! They are well mannered. They know better than to hurt an old gentleman.'

'How can I be sure of that?' whimpered the old man. 'Oh, oh, if I toss you down a piece of string, will you tie them up together?'

'Well, if it pleases you, I'll do that,' said Daniel.

And he laughed.

Then the old man tossed down a ball of red string. And Daniel tied one end of it to the dog's collar and the other end to the horse's halter, thinking to himself, 'What a foolish old man. As if the animals couldn't snap the string any moment if they wished to. But there, the poor old fellow's gone a bit crazy with age, I reckon.'

And he stood under the tree and held out his arms. 'Come along down now, little grandfather,' he said.

Then the old man came slithering down out of the tree, and Daniel caught him and set him gently before the fire. He didn't seem a bit grateful. Now he was moaning and groaning again: 'Oh, how hungry I am, how hungry!'

'And I have bread and cheese enough for two, and a bottle of good red wine,' said Daniel. 'So now you can eat your fill, and we'll take turn and turn about with the bottle.'

And they sat down one on each side of the fire, and began to eat and drink.

Daniel, being very hungry himself, didn't at first take much notice of the old man, except to reflect that his manners were not exactly gentlemanly, for he was snatching at the food, and tipping the bottle over his mouth to drink in an unpleasantly greedy fashion. 'But there,' he said to himself, 'the poor old fellow is half starved, so what else could one expect?' And then, happening to glance at him across the fire, he was truly startled.

'Why – old gentleman!' he gasped. 'You – you are surely growing bigger!'

'Oh no, no, no,' chuckled the old man. 'Not growing bigger, oh no – just getting nice and warm!'

'Oh well, I suppose the firelight's playing tricks with my eyes,' said Daniel. 'But what a truly hideous old thing he is!' he thought. 'Best not to look at him.'

And he went on eating.

But somehow he couldn't help glancing from time to time at the old man. And now he was sure that he was not mistaken. He *was* growing bigger. Every moment he was increasing in size; and what had been but a shrivelled little old bit of a body when he came down from the tree was now as big as Daniel himself – nay, bigger. And still he went on growing: now he was as big as an elephant, and still he went on growing. Now he was as big as the biggest tree in the forest, and still he went on growing . . . And he rose up and leaned over the fire with murder in his eyes.

'Hold him, my horse, hold him, my dog!' cried Daniel.

Alas, alas, neither horse nor dog could move. That little bit of red string held them fast.

The horse neighed, the dog barked. The old man stretched out his long, long leg: one kick of his huge bare foot for the dog, another kick of his huge bare foot for the horse. What happened? They crumbled into ashes.

And then, ah then, one last kick of that huge bare foot for Daniel . . . And he, too, crumbled into ashes. The huge old man gave such a shriek of laughter as set every tree in the forest quivering. And he danced on the fire with those huge bare feet till the flames died down, and the fire went out, and all was darkness.

And far away, at the cross roads where Mark and Daniel had parted, after thrusting their knives into the bark of the oak tree, one of the knives – the one that was Daniel's – fell clattering to the ground . . .

'We will meet under this oak in a year's time.' Mark, though well pleased with his job as coachman to the noble lord, remembered the words he had spoken before he had parted with Daniel at the cross roads, exactly a year ago. So he said a polite goodbye to the noble lord, thanked him for his kindness, and with a year's wages in his pocket, whistled to his dog, jumped on to his horse, and rode back to the cross roads. And there what did he see? His own knife still planted firmly in the oak, but Daniel's knife lying on the ground.

'Oh, brother Daniel, brother Daniel!' he cried. 'What can have happened to you?'

And he swung his horse round, and followed by his dog, set off at a gallop on the road to the right – the road that Daniel had taken a year ago.

All day he rode, and came at sunset to the moor on the edge of the forest. And here, pausing to look about him, he noticed that his dog was behaving in a strange manner. He was running round in circles, sniffing here, and sniffing there; and then he came hurrying to Mark with something in his mouth.

What was that something? A cast off horseshoe. And why should the dog be bringing him that horseshoe, unless by his keen scent he had recognised it?

'Brother Daniel,' thought Mark, 'certainly you have been here before me. And maybe you rested here for the night, brother; and maybe some of these ashes are the ashes from a fire that you lit. So what can I do better, brother, than follow your example?'

Well, he got down from his horse, hobbled it, left it to graze, and set about collecting wood and lighting a fire. And then he sat down with his back against the beech tree, just as Daniel had done, took meat and bread and a bottle of wine out of his knapsack, and began to eat his supper.

'O-oh how cold I am, how c-cold!' Up in the beech tree a whimpering voice. Mark looked up. What did he see? A little old man in a white shirt sitting hunched among the branches of the tree.

'Yes, old gentleman, the night is cold,' he said. 'But I have a good fire going. Why not come down and warm yourself?'

'No, no, *no*. Your horse will kick me, your dog will bite me!'

Mark laughed. 'My horse is hobbled, old gentleman, and my dog only bites my enemies. You have nothing to fear from either of them.'

'I am afraid, I am afraid,' whimpered the old man. 'Will you tie them together, if I give you a bit of string?'

Mark laughed again. 'If it will make you feel more comfortable, old gentleman, why certainly.'

Then the old man tossed down a ball of red string. But Mark, glancing up as he caught that string, saw something so hideously evil in the old man's expression, that he thought, 'Oh ho, old gentleman, I'm not trusting you, for I verily believe you are a fiend!' And getting up, he spoke softly to his dog, sauntered over to his horse, and all unperceived by the old man, tucked the ball of red string into his pocket, and tied horse and dog together with a piece of string of his own.

Meanwhile the old man had scrambled down from the tree, and seated himself by the fire. Mark came back to the fire, sat down opposite him, and opened his knapsack.

'Meat, sir?'

'Aye.'

'Bread, sir?'

'Aye.'

'A draught from the bottle, sir?'

'Aye.'

How he was snatching at the food, how he was gobbling, with what noisy gulps he was swallowing down the wine! Mark watched him with mixed feelings, part amused, part disgusted . . . And then suddenly he gasped.

'Old gentleman, you are growing bigger!'

'Well, maybe I am,' chuckled the old man. 'It's eating as does it.'

'Then I think you have eaten enough,' said Mark, 'if that's the way it takes you. Why, bless my soul, you are as big as my horse, nay bigger, you – you are as big as an elephant, you – you – Nay, hands off!' For now the Spectre (because that's what he was), towering to a prodigious height, was leaning over the fire with murder in his eyes.

'Hold him, my dog, hold him, my horse!' shouted Mark.

'Ho! Ho!' shrieked the Spectre. 'No use to call on *them*; my red string holds them fast.'

'The red string is in my pocket,' said Mark. 'I am not such a fool as you think! Ah ha, here they come. Don't you dare to move, old fellow, you best mind your manners if life is dear to you!'

The horse leaped, the dog pounced. The horse had the Spectre by the neck, the dog had him by one foot. Now he was shrinking, shrinking, shrinking; until from the giant he had been a moment ago, he was now but a shrivelled little old man again. And still horse and dog held him fast, and he was shrieking for mercy.

'Let me go,' he shrieked. 'Bid your animals loose me. I have gold, I tell you, gold, gold, I will give you gold!'

'I do not want your gold,' said Mark, 'I want my brother. His knife has fallen from the oak tree at the cross roads, so I know that he's met with misfortune. My dog has found a cast off shoe of my brother's horse here among the ashes, so that I know he has been here before me. What have you done with him? If you have killed him, I will now kill you. If you have spared his life, I will spare yours.'

'He is dust and ashes,' said the Spectre sulkily. 'How can I raise up dust and ashes?'

In a rage Mark drew his sword. He was about to strike the Spectre when he screamed out, 'No, no, no! You shall have your brother again! Somewhere among those heaps of ashes are *his* ashes. Go, gather up those ashes handful by handful, throw them over your left shoulder and say, "Rise up, dust and ashes! What I am now, what my horse and my dog are now, that may you also be." Then they will rise up, oh, they will rise up, men, dogs, and horses, and your brother will rise up with the rest. But you have promised to spare me, and so there is one pile of ashes that you must leave untouched – that little pile over there by itself under the big stone. For those are the ashes of a warrior king, and as I cast him down he cried out, "When *I* rise up, if ever that should be, may *you* lie down in my place." Oh, oh, I am afraid of that warrior king, I do not want to become dust and ashes! I do *not*, I tell you!' he shrieked.

'You should have thought of that before, old scoundrel,' said Mark. And he left him, still powerless in the hold of his horse and his dog, and went from ash pile to ash pile, gathering up the ashes handful by handful, throwing them over his left shoulder, and ever repeating as he did so, the same words, 'Rise up, dust and ashes! As I am now, may you also be.'

Then from each pile of ashes rose up a living being: travellers both of low and high degree, men and women, horses and dogs – dazed looking people, bewildered animals – and among them Mark's brother Daniel, and Daniel's horse, and Daniel's dog.

'Brother Mark,' said Daniel, 'what has happened? How came you here? I – I do not remember – '

'Time enough to remember by and by,' answered Mark. 'First I must finish my work.' And he hurried to the little pile of ashes under the big stone.

'Rise up, dust and ashes,' he said, 'what I am now, may you also be.'

The ashes stirred, the ashes gathered themselves together, they lifted themselves from the ground, they took shape. What were they now? No longer dust and ashes, but a tall and handsome young king. And as those ashes rose up, so the Spectre, who was still held firmly in the grip of Mark's horse and dog, shuddered, shrivelled, and fell into dust.

Then the air resounded with shouts of triumph: 'The old man is gone! The Spectre has been turned to ashes! And we are alive, alive again!' Men and women, youths and maidens, old and young, surrounding Mark, calling down blessings upon him, kissing his hands, kneeling to kiss his feet. And so in small companies, they mounted their horses and rode away, leaving the handsome young king and Mark and Daniel, and their horses and dogs, standing by a little pile of dust . . . all that was left of the Spectre.

'A sorry tale, but with a happy ending, thanks to you, my good sir,' said the handsome young king, smiling at Mark. 'Now I – oh so joyfully – will return to my kingdom. And you?'

'I think my brother and I will go home,' said Mark with a tired smile. 'I think we have had quite enough of adventure.'

'And what will you do when you get home?' asked the handsome young king.

'Go back to our fishing, I suppose,' said Mark. 'And maybe, if we work hard and put by every penny we earn, perhaps some day we may save up enough to marry our sweethearts. But that is as fate wills,' he added. And he sighed.

'Nay,' said the young king. 'What do you take me for – an ungrateful wretch? You shall go home, yes. But you shall not stay there. You shall tell your sweethearts the whole story. And if they are willing, as no doubt they will be, you shall bring them to my court. I will send a coach and horses for them. And we will hold a double wedding, the merriest that can be. And surely after that we shall all live happily, for I have work for such men as you.'

So that's what happened. The young king returned to his kingdom, the brothers jumped on to their horses and rode home, each one followed by his faithful dog. They told their story to their sweethearts, and very soon the king's golden coach arrived outside their cottage door. The girls got into the coach, Daniel and Mark mounted their horses, the dogs ran behind, and merrily, merrily they all set out for the king's court to hold a double wedding, and live happily ever after.

And as the whole company, coach, riders, horses and dogs, passed along the coast road, by the bay where the brothers had a year ago cast in their net and caught the little rainbow coloured fish, that little fish put his head up out of the water, and cried, 'Didn't I tell you that if you spared my life I would make your fortunes? And haven't I done it? Hip, hip, hurrah!'

18 · Goralasi and the Spectres

There was a man who went by the name of Goralasi the Fool, and to be sure he was not very bright-witted. But he had a neighbour called Didipapa who was sensible and clever. And Didipapa helped Goralasi out of many a scrape that his foolishness got him into.

Well now, one day these two men went with some people from another village up into the mountains for a feast. There they lit a fire and roasted yams, which they mashed up with grated coconuts to make them more tasty. And after they had feasted they danced and sang, and made merry until sunset.

Then they packed up to go home, not wishing to be benighted among the mountains.

They still had a pile of food left over, so they divided it among themselves, and each one carried his share in a clam shell – a big oval-shaped shell with a lid to it, which makes a very pretty dish.

So, singing and laughing, they all went down the mountain together for a little way; and then Didipapa and Goralasi took one path, and the other men took another path, each taking the most direct way back to their villages.

Well, Goralasi and Didipapa hadn't gone very far when – did you ever? – there right in the middle of their path stood a Spectre. The path was narrow; there was no possibility of getting round that Spectre. So Didipapa put down his clam shell and began to say a prayer. Surely that would drive the Spectre away!

But it didn't drive the Spectre away. That Spectre began praying in his turn.

Didipapa said another prayer.

The Spectre said another prayer.

Didipapa said a third prayer.

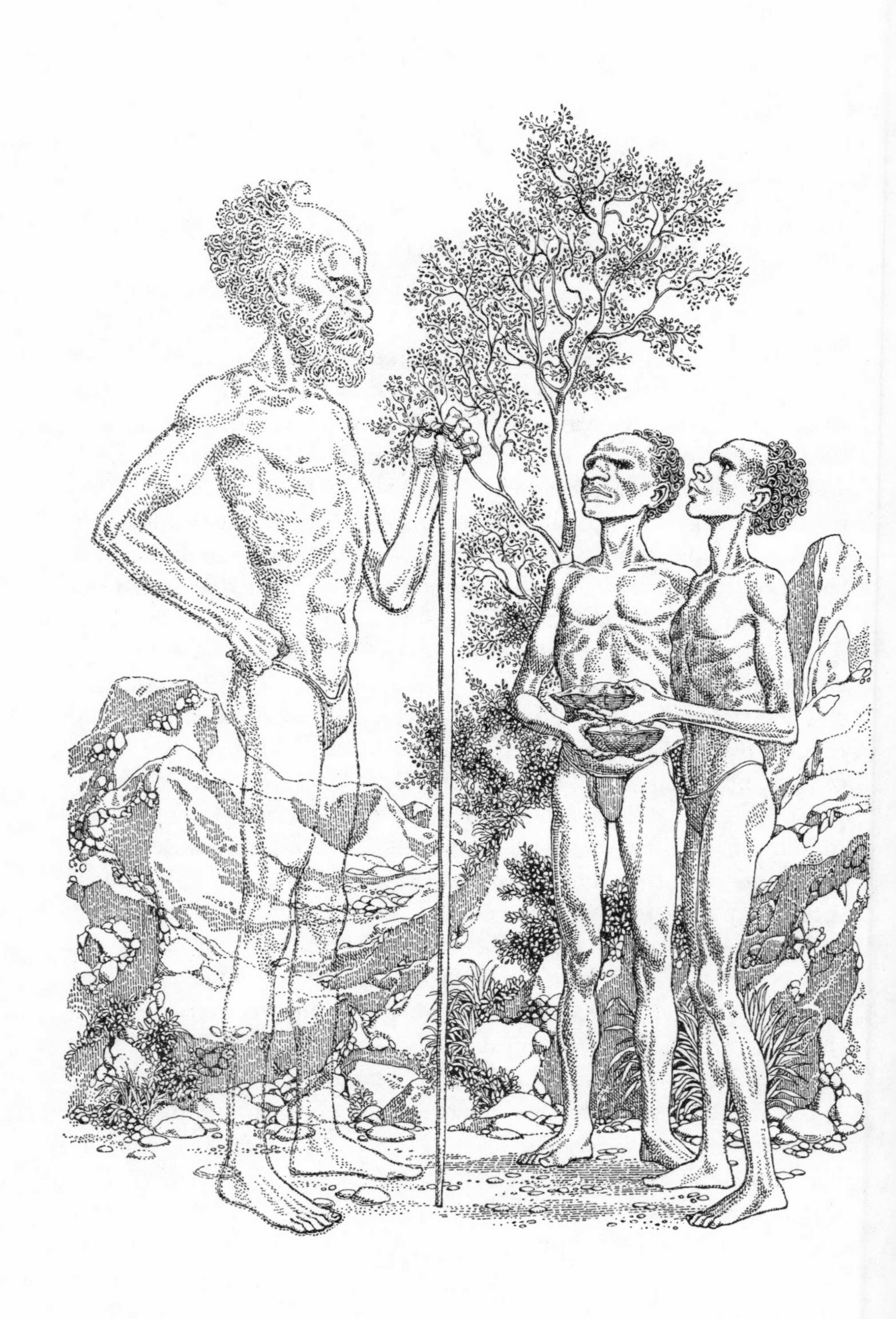

The Spectre said a third prayer.

No, there was no getting rid of the Spectre that way. So Didipapa whispered to Goralasi, 'Take your shell, dodge round the Spectre and be off down to the village. I'll say yet one more prayer, and if the Spectre begins to pray again, I'll take my chance of getting past him.'

Now that was very kind and brave of Didipapa, as I'm sure you'll agree.

Goralasi didn't need telling twice: clutching his clam shell he dodged round the Spectre and took to his heels. He ran, ran, and all the time he was looking for a place to hide, because he was afraid the Spectre might come after him and catch him up. Well, by and by he saw a clump of long grasses growing by the side of the path, and under these grasses he crept. Now his head and body were hidden, but his legs were sticking out, plain to see. And he had put his clam shell down in the middle of the path, and that was plain to see also. Well – what else could you expect from a fool?

Up above on the path, Didipapa and the Spectre were still facing one another, and Didipapa was saying prayers with all his might, when the Spectre suddenly turned and glided away down the path after Goralasi. He came to where Goralasi was hiding, and saw the clam shell lying on the ground, and Goralasi's legs sticking out from under the grasses. He took hold of Goralasi's legs, pulled him out from under the grasses, and jerked him on to his feet.

'Take up your shell,' he said, 'and come with me.'

'Where – where are we g-going?' stammered Goralasi.

'Never you mind,' said the Spectre. 'Come.'

And he led Goralasi up the mountain again, and along another path, and round the mountain and down again, going at such a speed that Goralasi became quite giddy, and lost all sense of where he was.

Then he saw bright lights ahead, and they came into a valley where a great many wood fires were burning, and a throng of people were cooking their evening meal – men, women and children, and all of them were Spectres.

Now our Spectre told Goralasi to stand behind a tree and keep quiet. And when Goralasi had done this, our Spectre went over to the fires to join the others. The Spectres left their cooking and crowded round him. They were sniff, sniff, sniffing.

'You smell of Man,' they cried. 'Where is that Man? Show him to us!'

'Before I show him to you, you must promise not to hurt him,' said our Spectre.

'No, no, we won't hurt him,' cried the other Spectres.

So then our Spectre brought Goralasi out from behind the tree, and the Spectres crowded round him, feeling him all over, patting him with their frail white hands, laughing and exclaiming, 'Oh, isn't he tough, isn't he rough, isn't he thick, isn't he a great hulky-bulky absurd awkward creature!'

Goralasi wasn't liking it at all. And suddenly he shouted, 'Anyway I'm alive, and that's more than any of you can boast of being! And if I *am* tough and rough, that's better than being a thing one could poke one's finger through!'

So then the Spectres laughed, and told him to come to the fire and share their supper with them.

Goralasi stayed with the Spectres for three days. They made a pet of him, treating him as if he had been some kind of big dog. And Goralasi was enjoying it. But on the fourth morning some men, to whom the land belonged, came up to see to their plantations. Then the Spectres made themselves invisible, and they must have made Goralasi invisible also: at any rate the planters didn't see him. And though Goralasi called to them, they didn't hear him. But somehow the sight of those men made Goralasi unhappy, and he told the Spectres he would like to go home.

'You see I don't belong here,' he said, 'and though you are very kind, I think I like my own people best.'

'Well, if that's so,' said the Spectres, 'we won't keep you.'

Then they gave Goralasi back his clam shell, and loaded him up with all manner of good things: bananas, sweet potatoes, yams and even vegetable marrows, which they took from the plantations of the men who owned the land. They strung all these things together and hung them over Goralasi's shoulders. He was so laden down that he could scarcely walk; he had to carry everything himself, the Spectres were floating along round him without carrying anything. And when he lagged, they were urging him on with little whistlings and coaxings, just as if, as I have said, he had been a pet dog.

In the early morning they came in sight of Goralasi's home village. And then suddenly all the Spectres vanished. And as they vanished they were calling out very softly, 'Goodbye, Goralasi, be a good boy, Goralasi, and give our respects to Didipapa. He's a fine fellow is Didipapa! But you're not a bad fellow yourself, Goralasi.'

So their voices grew fainter and fainter, and then they were gone. And Goralasi stumbled on into the village, to find himself surrounded by a crowd of his own people.

'What, Goralasi! Where have you been all this time? And, pah, Goralasi, how dirty you are!'

No good Goralasi trying to tell them about the Spectres. They wouldn't believe him. They said he had been dreaming, though they were glad enough to accept the good things he had brought. 'And we're not asking any questions as to where or how you got them, Goralasi,' they said. 'Only do go down into the sea and wash – you're not fit to be seen!'

Goralasi felt like crying. He did so want the people to believe his story. But he went into the sea, and had a thorough wash. And then he felt better.

'After all, I *did* have a good time with the Spectres,' he said to Didipapa.

19 · The Lake

The lake lay just outside the village. It was not very big, to be sure, but its waters were clear and bright. And on sunny days, and on moonlit nights, those waters sparkled so prettily that the village people said, 'See how our lake shines, just as if it was filled with gold!'

And when they had said that a great many times, when the grandfathers and grandmothers had said it, and the fathers and mothers had said it, and the boys and girls had said it, the people began to think that what they said was true. And now it was no longer 'just as if our lake was filled with gold', but 'our lake *is* filled with gold – or at least there is gold at the bottom of it!'

And since they were greedy people they added, 'If there is gold under our lake, well then we're going to have it!'

And there they were, men and women, boys and girls, jumping into the lake, and splashing and diving to try and get up that gold.

The lake had no peace day or night, and this annoyed it very much. So what did it do? It called its fish together, and rose up

into the air and flew away. The people watched it as it flew, high, high under the clouds, and they said, 'Ah ha! *Now* the bed of the lake is laid bare, and *now* we can pick up its gold!'

So they took sacks and buckets and baskets and scrambled down into the bed of the lake. What did they find there? Nothing but mud and snakes and toads. And they sulked, because now there was nowhere for their cattle to drink, and they had to go trudging to and fro to outlying streams to fetch water.

And what was the lake doing? It was flying, flying, and looking down on the world to find some place where it might rest. It was flying by day, it was flying by night. And one bright morning it saw a pretty little town, lying snugly in a hollow between two hills.

'Ah,' thought the lake, 'that is the place for me!'

And it floated gently down, and came to rest in a field.

The townspeople were delighted when they saw the lake, because they had always been short of water. They ran out into the field, and danced and sang, 'Welcome to you, dear lake! Welcome, welcome! Now we will plant young trees around you to cool your face; and if you are willing we will bring our horses and cattle to drink of your waters!'

'Yes, you may do that,' said the lake. 'But one thing I pray you *not* to do. Do not come splashing and diving into my waters in search of treasure; for that would be greedy of you, and not at all pleasant for me.'

'No, no, dear lake, we promise not to disturb you,' said the people.

Then they brought trees and planted them all round the lake. And on festival days they hung garlands of flowers on the trees. And the lake took the reflections of these garlands into its bright waters, and was very pleased.

By and by a Spook came to live in the lake, and sometimes on moonlit nights the Spook would come out of the water and sit chatting with the people. It was a very gentle creature, and its voice was like the patter of little waves when they run in on shore. And when it went down into the lake again it would call out '*Catch!*' And up from the bright waters of the lake would flash a piece of gold. It took to doing this on the night of every full moon. Then the townspeople gathered round the lake, and one or other of them would catch that piece of gold. They were very fair-minded, they took the gold in turns. And so in the course of years everyone became rich and lived happily, blessing the day when the lake sailed down out of the sky and came to rest in their field.

20 · *Strange Visitors*

On a stormy night, a warrior, one of the Emperor's captains, sat alone in his room, reading by candlelight. He had green eyes and a bold expression. Frequently he had been heard to say 'Fear? What is fear?'

The rain drummed on the roof and gusts of wind lashed the bamboos against the walls of the house.

Suddenly through the closed door there came a most curious object. It looked like the stump of a tree wrapped in black sack-cloth. And it came jumping across the room, and sat down on the floor between the Captain and the fireplace.

The Captain took no notice. He went on reading.

By and by another curious-looking object, just like the first one, sprang through the closed door, jumped across the room, and sat down by the first one.

The Captain took no notice. He went on reading.

Then a third curious-looking object, just like the other two, came through the closed door, jumped across the room, and sat down by the others.

The Captain went on reading.

And there was silence, except for the roaring of the wind, and the drumming of the rain on the roof.

But now the three strange Shapes in black sackcloth began to move. They came so close to the Captain that they were pressing against his feet.

The Captain moved his chair a little way back, and went on reading.

Again the three Shapes pressed forward; again the Captain moved back his chair. This went on for some time: the Shapes moving forward, the Captain still reading, but moving back with his chair, until there he was right up against the wall. And then he clapped his book shut, and said angrily, 'Who are you, that you dare to push me about like this in my own room?'

Then the first Shape croaked out, 'I'm hungry!'

And the second Shape croaked out, 'We're hungry, hungry!'

And the third Shape croaked out, 'Hungry! *Hungry!* HUNGRY!'

'Well, why didn't you mention that before?' said the Captain. 'I've some food in the cupboard.'

And he got up to go to the cupboard.

But the first Shape croaked out, 'It's you we're going to eat!'

And the second Shape croaked out, 'Yes-s, you, *you*!'

And the third Shape croaked out, 'Yes-s-ss, you, *you*, YOU!'

'Oh, are you?' shouted the Captain.

He doubled up his fist and struck a blow at the first Shape.

But his fist went clean through it.

He struck a blow at the second Shape.

But his fist went clean through it.

He struck a blow at the third Shape. But his fist went clean through it. And something caught him by the leg and tumbled him to the floor. He got such a knock on the back of his head that he lost his senses . . .

When he came to himself, the wind had died down, the rain had stopped, the three Shapes had vanished, and the room was very, very quiet.

The Captain scrambled to his feet. He put a hand to his head, which was aching.

'May the good spirits protect us all from any more of such visitors!' he said.

And he took up his book and went on reading.

21 · *The Dance of the Spectres*

It was May Day. But the king of the country had died the night before, and now prayers were being said for his soul in all the churches. Certainly it was no moment for making merry! But the young folk of the capital city had been looking forward to setting up their maypole, and dancing round it, as they had always done, and as their parents, and their grandparents, and their great-grandparents had done, as far back as the history of the country would take them.

'It's too bad, it's just too bad!' the young folk said. 'People are forever being born and dying! Why should we be robbed of our pleasure? The king was old, and we are young. May Day comes but once a year . . . ' And so on, and so on.

Well, the long and the short of it was that these young people went at dawn into the wood, and chose out a fine slender beech tree. They cut the tree down, lopped off its branches, carried it to a smooth meadow outside the city, decorated it with ribbons and streamers, set it up, and went off to their breakfasts well pleased with themselves, and agreeing to meet in the early afternoon to hold their dance round the maypole as usual.

And they did meet in the early afternoon. Yes, there they all were, the girls in their best dresses, the lads in all their finery, old Martin with his fiddle, young Pietro with his pipes, little Cosimo with his drum. Now strike up fiddle, pipes and drum – here we go, merrily dancing round and round, merrily dancing hand in hand!

Does the sun shine, does the breeze blow softly? Yes, for a little while. But then clouds cover the sky, dark, gloomy clouds, blotting out the sun. The soft breeze becomes a strong breeze, and the strong breeze becomes a whirlwind. Ho, you musicians, it is time to pack up! Ho, young men and maidens it is time to hie you home!

'No, no, *no*, we are having such fun! We will dance a little longer, just a little longer!'

But now there is a flash of lightning, now a clap of thunder; now the rain comes pelting down. The musicians pack up in a hurry, and in a hurry make for home. But what is this? The young folk are still dancing – it seems they cannot stop. And indeed they cannot stop: round they must go, and round, and round, and now their faces are drawn with terror, and their hair whirls about their heads, as round they go, and round they go, and round they go again.

The sun sets amid a tumult of storm clouds: now it is evening, now it is black night – and in the darkness the unseen lads and maidens are still whirling round and round, in a dance that has no end.

Dawn, morning, noonday, afternoon, evening – another day drawing to its close, and still those lads and maidens are dancing, dancing. The town is empty of people, everyone has rushed out to the meadow. 'Stop, stop, you fools!' the people are shouting. But still the crazy dance goes on.

And then – oh horror! – the dancers begin to disappear! First their feet sink into the ground, then their legs sink, then their bodies. Now it is only their heads that are left above ground, and round the maypole go those heads, bobbing, jerking, the mouths wide open as if they were screaming with terror, and yet uttering no sound. And now the faces too have disappeared, and all that is left are tufts of hair, blown this way and that way by the wind, but still whirling round and round.

The mothers of the young folk are sobbing with terror; the fathers of the young folk are dashing forward, trying to get a grasp of those tufts of hair, and by them drag the young folk up on to solid ground. But their hands are grabbing at empty air; and slowly, slowly, even those tufts of hair vanish, and the maypole vanishes; and all that is left is the smooth green grass of the meadow.

Yes, all those pretty maidens and stalwart youths have disappeared, and the maypole also has sunk into the ground.

Is that the end of the story? No, it isn't.

Wailing and in bitter grief, the townsfolk return home. The church bell tolls, the priest is offering up prayers for the souls of the dancers. There is mourning in the city for many a day.

But the years pass, life must go on, other boys and girls are born and are growing up. The priest who was young when he offered up those prayers for the dancers, is now an old man. And on a May Day some thirty years later, this old priest is taking a walk in the meadow, and meditating, as he is in the habit of meditating, on all the happenings of his long life.

Now he is weary, and he sits down to rest on a log near to the place where the maypole once stood.

He is almost asleep, when he hears a rustling in the grass, and feels a gentle breeze blowing across his face. He opens his eyes. What does he see?

Out of the ground rise a crowd of feet, some in such shoes as lads wear on Sundays, some in girls' dainty slippers.

And a wind rises and moans over the meadow, saying '*Hush, hush!*'

Then up out of the ground rise legs, some clothed in pantaloons, some in girls' muslin skirts. And the legs place themselves on top of the feet.

And the wind blows over the meadow, murmuring, '*Hush, hush!*'

Then out of the ground rise bodies, armless bodies, young men's bodies, and maidens' bodies. And the bodies place themselves on top of the legs.

And the wind blows over the meadow, murmuring '*Hush, hush!*'

Then out of the ground rise hands and arms, young men's hands and arms, maidens' hands and arms, and join themselves on to the bodies.

And the wind blows over the meadow, murmuring '*Hush, hush!*'

Then out of the ground rise necks and heads: young men's necks and heads, maidens' necks and heads. And the necks and heads join themselves on to the bodies.

Now there they stand, a ghostly company of spectres, the spectres of youths and maidens.

And as if blown by the wind this spectral company moves over

to the place where the maypole once stood. A spectral maypole rises out of the ground. The spectral company of youths and maidens join hands and begin to dance. Round the maypole they go, and round they go, and round and round again. But crystal tears are filling the eyes and trickling down the cheeks of the maidens, and the faces of the youths are sad, oh sad! But round they must go, and round they must go, *fast*, *fast*, *faster* – until they are all merged together in a whirling mass from which come sobs and moans and bitter crying.

The sun sets, twilight falls over the meadow. Now the spectral dance is dim to see, but still it goes on. The moon rises: the spectral dance is bright to see again, and still the spectres whirl round and round amid sobs and groans and bitter crying.

Until, far away, but sharp to hear, comes the crowing of a cock. A new day dawns, and with the dawn the maypole vanishes; and slowly, slowly the spectres sink into the ground, first their feet, then their legs, then their bodies, and last of all their heads. Now in the place where they were dancing there is only the green grass glistening with drops of dew.

The old priest gets to his feet and crosses himself.

'And is this to be their fate until Doomsday?' he asks.

'Yes, until Doomsday,' answers a voice out of the clouds.

'And is there *no* hope, no forgiveness for them?' cries the old priest.

'After Doomsday comes hope, and after Doomsday comes forgiveness,' answers the voice out of the clouds.

22 · *Heaven Forbid!*

Well now, here's Peder Gudmund, who has been to town on business, and is riding home by moonlight. He is seated on the back of his good grey horse, and his big dog, Ollie, is running at the horse's heels. Peder is thinking that he has settled all his affairs to his own advantage; and surely that is enough to make any man feel comfortable in his mind. And he *is* comfortable in his mind, though the night is very dark, and he is crossing a moor that folk say is haunted by Spooks . . .

And hullo, hullo, *there* are the Spooks, a great company of them, big Spooks and little Spooks, and all as thin as muslin, so that you can see the back of them through the front of them.

What are those Spooks doing? They are bringing up great bags of gold out of a hole in the ground, and they are laying those bags out in a criss-cross pattern on the turf.

And as they are laying down the bags, so they are singing, in wavery quavery fluttering voices, that sound like breezes blowing through a field of rustling corn.

'A bag for me, and a bag for you, and a bag for Billie Bingels!' sing the Spooks.

'And a bag for Peder Gudmund!' shouts Peder.

And he jumps off his horse, snatches up one of the bags, and up on his horse again, and away to go at a gallop.

Well, he hasn't gone far when he hears a puffing and a panting and a *clip*, *clip*, *clipperty* behind him. And glancing over his shoulder, he sees a tiny little Spook with a long white beard, riding on a very small white horse, no bigger than a cat, and followed by a very small black dog, no bigger than a mouse.

'Wilt thou let *thy* horse fight with *my* horse?' shrills the tiny little Spook.

'Nay, heaven forbid!' shouts Peder.

And he gallops on.

'Then wilt thou let *thy* dog fight with *my* dog?' shrills the tiny little Spook.

'Nay, heaven forbid!' shouts Peder.

'Then wilt thou thyself fight with me, little as I am?' shrills the very small Spook.

'Nay, heaven forbid!' shouts Peder.

And he whips up his horse and gallops on, *fast*, *fast*, *faster*.

Now the puffings and the pantings are dwindling away in the distance, and the little shrill voice has ceased to call. Peder reaches home, hurriedly stables his horse, and hurriedly carries his bag full of gold coins into the kitchen, locking the house door behind him.

'All's well that ends well,' says Peder.

But big dog Ollie sits in a corner and shivers.

Then comes a hissing and a storming outside. Rain falls in torrents, lightning flashes, thunder booms. So brilliant and so close are those flashes of lightning that the whole house seems to be ablaze. With every clap of thunder the house shudders, the crockery clatters down from the shelves, chairs are turning topsy-turvy. Peder can scarcely keep on his feet. He is clutching at the table; but the table is sliding from one end of the kitchen to the other. And big dog Ollie, crouched in his corner, is howling pitifully.

Frightened almost out of his wits, Peder snatches up the bag of treasure, and flings it out into the yard. Then the storm dies away.

And there is a great silence.

And out of the silence comes a shrill little voice.

'Thou hast still enough!' shrills that little voice.

Peder went to bed. He didn't sleep very well. He was having nightmares.

Next morning, when he went downstairs, he saw big dog Ollie, standing in the kitchen, looking up at the dresser, and wagging his tail.

What was big dog Ollie looking at?

A beautiful large silver goblet, brimful of gold coins.

23 · *Ha! ha! ha!*

Once upon a time a young Spook got tired of living in Spook Land. So he changed himself into a beautiful red and black bird, and flew off into the world of men to seek adventure.

He flew, flew, flew, and came to a strip of moorland on the edge of a forest. Just where the forest ended and the moor began, there were some birch trees; and under the birch trees stood a young broom-binder.

The broom-binder was busy stripping the leaves off a pile of twigs he had cut from the birch trees; and he had taken off his jacket and his boots, and laid them beside the rope with which, by and by, he was going to tie up the twigs, when he had stripped them bare of their leaves.

'Now we will have some fun!' thought the red and black bird.

And he flew down, perched himself on a low branch of one of the birch trees, and gave a loud laugh. '*Ha! ha! ha!*'

The broom-binder looked up into the tree. 'Oh, what a beautiful bird! If I could catch him, I would take him home as a present for my little sweetheart!' thought the broom-binder.

So he stood on tiptoe, stretched out his hand, and made a grab at the bird.

'*Ha! ha! ha!*' laughed the bird, and flew up on to a higher branch.

The broom-binder climbed up after it.

'*Ha! ha! ha!*' laughed the bird, and flew up on to a yet higher branch.

The broom-binder climbed up after it.

'*Ha! ha! ha!*' laughed the bird.

Blast the bird – it was certainly mocking him! The broom-binder got angry. Now he was all the more determined to catch it.

But up and up the tree from one branch to another branch went the bird, and up and up went the broom-binder after it. And always as the broom-binder thought to catch hold of it, the bird laughed '*Ha! ha! ha!*' and flew on to a yet higher branch. Until it came to the topmost branch. And then – *Ha! ha! ha!* – that bird spread out its red and black wings and flew away.

The broom-binder climbed down from the tree . . . Where was he? Not on the strip of moorland where he had left his jacket and

his boots, and his rope, and his axe, and the twigs he had been stripping, but on a lonely wilderness of rocks and great stones – and which way to turn to get home he simply didn't know.

The sun had set too, and the whole world seemed wrapped in a grey twilight. And through the twilight he heard, but far off and very, very faintly, the voice of the bird, laughing '*Ha! ha! ha!*'

'Well, I've learned better than to follow *you*, at any rate!' said the broom-binder.

And he turned in the opposite direction, stumbling over the rocks and stones that kept cropping up under his feet, as if determined to throw him down.

And thankful indeed he was when he saw, twinkling ahead of him, the lights of his own village, which he reached at last, and came to his own little cottage, and cooked himself some supper, and went to bed. But still in his dreams he was chasing that red and black bird, and hearing its mocking laughter, '*Ha! ha! ha!*'

Next morning he went again to the heath to collect his boots and his jacket and his axe and his rope and the cut-down birch twigs, which now lay scattered all over the place as if someone had been playing pitch-and-toss with them. Well, he had gathered up those twigs into a neat bundle, and tied them together with the rope, and was just heaving the bundle on to his back, when, from the top of the birch tree, came that mocking laughter, '*Ha! ha! ha!*'

The broom-binder straightened himself, looked up into the tree, and shook his fist. 'Be off with you, whoever you may be! Be off to where you belong, before I heave a stone at you!' he shouted.

'*Ha! ha! ha!*' laughed the bird.

And it spread its red and black wings, and flew back to Spook Land.